# SERIOUS

CONNOR MILLER

For L

# CONTENTS

# FOREWORD

Miller's *Serious* is the dark and plotless confession of a young man with a fist-shaped heart and a hunger for momentum, spark, something bankable, and someone to love with a centripetal love. Our narrator is also uncentered, so much so that the narrative voice is shifted to the second person, to "you." All the action befalls, demoralizes, arouses, troubles, vitalizes "you." "You walk a block, pretending your right foot is deformed, curved inward" (Chapter 5). "You sometimes feel like you are your own teddy bear" (Chapter 8). "Claire wants to marry you" (Chapter 9).

I trust our dissociated narrator. I believe his reportage is honest. Consider the first chapter of *Serious*, which brims with named characters: Ben, Jan, James, Mia, Rebecca, Pierre, Parish, Hannah, Kevin, Haley, Brian, Russell, Claire, Robert, Robin, Heather, Andrew, Michael, Nate, Kai, Jacob, Uncle James, David, Grace, and Samantha. Twenty-four names in the span of the first chapter. This, by the way, is merely the list of named characters; the list of persons altogether includes the unnamed father, mother, therapist, creative writing teacher, and so on. And the list should include famous names mentioned, e.g., Samuel Beckett, Asher Roth, Anais Nin, and so on.

Yet, it never feels crowded. This first chapter, as with every chapter, moves memory-like from one person to the next, never introducing characters for the sake of characters, but for the sake of approximating actual experience, where webs of people tangle up together and time is subordinated to nonlinear consciousness. Flashback, anecdote, envisioned future, and Instagram post, among other devices, turn time into another character without a center, without a home. I say "without a home," because the concept of home, here surfacing and there submerging, seems to me fundamental for this narrator.

What is home for the narrator? The most explicit musings on home come in the first half of the first chapter: "You read Thich Nhat Hanh who tells you that you must make a home in your heart before you invite others in, you liken your heart to your apartment. If you can make a home, a good home, a loving home, you can then share it with others who need it. [...] You want to be brave with people, to furnish your heart and invite them to sleep over, to eat your food, and to bring their own furniture, to share your hearts until the world is at home with you."

Heart, body, physical closeness, sleeping together, sharing food—these are some elements of the homeward pulse under the skin of events. Without these elements, "Everything feels so flimsy, you wish you had something solid to hold, like a body" (last line of that chapter).

But home is not anywhere in particular, and this creates indecision, ambivalence, push-and-pull, goings-and-returnings. The narrator calls his parents every weekend, kindling a sense of home. The narrator seems to openly suppress his worry that the Bay Area, the place of family and oldest friends, will be both his starting and finishing line. I felt as though I was sampling the private diary of the prodigal son, but a modern prodigal son, one who returns home only to re-lose his sense of home: "In a couple of months you are living at home, back in the Bay Area, hiding bottles of whiskey under your pillow." This is the cyclical prodigal son. Home is always everywhere else. This is signaled in the comment of his Bay Area friend Kevin: "What the fuck are you doing here?"

Oscillation, variability, disequilibria—the narrator embodies so much of that going and returning and never-quite-settling. There is uncertainty between some A and some B. "You don't know whether to live with it [being a writer] forever, or to banish it from your life completely."

And: "Sometimes you think that writing is antiquated. Other times you think it is essential. Both times you are too impatient to sit and figure out which one of these statements is actually true." And later: "There are days you are worried that you are an idiot [...] Then, there are days that you feel like Donald-Fucking-Draper. It's hard to figure out which of these realities is true." Again, A or B? A or B? Home or adventure. Bay Area as home or Bay Area as cage?—or simultaneously home and cage? You can sympathize with the narrator when he says of his writing: "Most of what you write is a manifestation of worry."

His romantic relationships, as possible places of home, of resettlement, also participate in the ambivalent movements of the homeward narrator. The narrator reflects on his high school romances: "Now, you slowly become aware of how much of high school was clouded by denial. Denial about about who liked you, who didn't, who were your friends, who loved you." I read this and thought: this has continued beyond high school. The narrator is still clouded, perhaps not now by juvenile denial, but by its adult forms. Or clouded by the actions of others, e.g., "you know that friends-of-girlfriends will only like you for as long as she [the girlfriend] likes you." I found that sentence so brutal in its diagnosis of the contractual nature of so much modern friendship. Elsewhere, the narrator expresses his own cloudiness in romance: "Even if you care, you must grunt and not look at your phone and pretend you aren't interested." That is the embodiment of a denial.

The narrator is nomadic, uncertainly nihilistic, and fearful (e.g., of his health, particularly and most curiously, of the health of his heart). As he says, in one of my favorite sentences, "constants are few." This is echoed later when he says, "Again, you have to think, focus, to identify beautiful moments. There are few." So, constants are few and beautiful moments are few. How rare, then, is something that is simultaneously constant and beautiful?

You get the overwhelming impression that, for this narrator, the beautiful constant is too rare to find, let alone make into an abiding home.

Friedrich Nietzsche wrote: "To those human beings who are of any concern to me I wish suffering, desolation, sickness, ill-treatment, indignities—I wish that they should not remain unfamiliar with profound self-contempt, the torture of self-mistrust, the wretchedness of the vanquished: I have no pity for them, because I wish them the only thing that can prove today whether one is worth anything or not—that one endures." (The Will to Power, p 481)

Despite the scarcity of constants and abundance of dead-ends, disruptions, and doubts, the narrator of Serious endures; he is "strong in the broken places," to steal a line from Hemingway. The narrator performs this strength of the broken places through the spidered mirror of a fragmentary confession.

Or using another image, I imagine *Serious* as an ill-lit ocean shore spangled with innumerable, half-buried chips of seashell. Most seashells are washed up broken and worn-down; few collectors seek these fragments, especially fragments of the common shell types. But some collectors do gather the fragments, even of the common shells. Some gather them into a reliquary, a place for holy objects. The message of this rare collector of the common is clear: each struggle in the sea deserves reverence.

— Jonathan van Belle
March 8, 2016

# 1

# SERIOUS

There is a moment when you realize that you need to "get serious", when things stop becoming funny and comfortable, and you stare at yourself in the mirror with the grim-face and think, "okay, this is it, this is where everything changes."

There is a moment where you stand in a parking lot with your friend Ben and he looks at you and asks you to punch him in the face and you do, as hard as you can, because you've seen at least two movies where punches to the face bring sudden clarity and all you want is sudden clarity.

You and Ben, in general, hate everything. You took up smoking this year, you have these bags under your eyes and you frequently consider arson. Ben seems to handle it a little bit better than you do, but Ben just wears *life* a little bit better than you do, which is why, perhaps, you are friends with him.

Ben is holding his jaw after you punch him in the face and rubs it gently, trying to figure out what exactly he is meant to learn from this experience. "That was good," he says quietly. "That was good."

And you are frustrated because you want him to punch you back in the face, but he is much taller and stronger than you and you have a belief that your bone structure is delicate (it may or may not be true, you have not broken any bones yet but you are kind of into the idea of maybe having someone snap your arm in half).

There is a moment where Ben will uppercut you, unexpectedly, in the same parking lot, without warning, and your teeth with smash together so hard that one of the teeth chips and you taste aluminum foil. And you will stagger back and taste blood and get very angry (you've been angry) because what if you bit off your tongue because of this? What if because Ben uppercutted you, you would never be able to speak normally again. But all that happened was your tooth chipped, and you spit out the sliver onto the sidewalk and feel the broken corner with your tongue (new and jagged) and you don't even think about dentistry or cost because now you, just like Ben, have the same thought echoing in your head: "That was good. That was good."

~

You are sitting in a bar with three friends. The four of you are leaning over an iPhone in the center of the table, waiting for Jan to text back. You are like generals in a war room, debating the course of action, trying to decide what combination of words will increase the likelihood that you will get laid. There is a rule you learned in high school is that you should never text back immediately (you must always seem busy), but now, as an adult, this is no longer a problem because a) you are always busy and b) you are sometimes so anxious about texting that you simply don't know what to say and choose to wait a couple hours after your emotions die down.

~

You are sitting in a bar with three friends and you are kind of angry because Jan might doing the same thing you are doing, calling shots with friends, the four of them fighting over what is the best course of action to take. The whole thing strikes you as preposterous, and you try to think of a better way to talk to her but there is no better way, this feels like it's going to be the only way you interact with people for the rest of your life.

~

There is a moment when she texts you and the table goes silent, because suddenly it's clear she's down to fuck, and no one really expected that. It was fun up until this moment, but now it is suddenly real, and you say "I have to go," because to dawdle here at the bar with James, Mia, and Rebecca, to dawdle here would be absurd.

~

3

So, in the street, you light up a cigarette and walk in the direction of her house, trying to brainstorm better ways of talking to people, wanting to curb-stomp your phone but knowing you simply can't.

~

There is a moment that you decide that for the rest of your life you will be an asshole. Funny enough, it is in your friend Pierre's apartment (as you may have noticed, in this hypothetical situation you have a lot of friends, but it does not help you feel less alone). Pierre is tired from his nine-to-five job, and he is cutting open a bagel and making polite conversation with you because you are his guest. Pierre tells you that the one thing he regrets was that he built this persona of being a "nice guy" and he isn't quite sure if that was the right decision. You are generally angry as an individual, and you may have been a nice guy at some point (like in middle school) but whenever you imagine these instances of you being "nice" (like opening the door for someone, or bringing soup to a girl you like), you are filled with a furious rage and you tell yourself you would never, ever do something like that again.

~

There is a moment when you are biking alone at midnight and your heart is skipping beats (imagine that you cannot go to the hospital, imagine that you do not have healthcare). You are deep in Southeast Portland and it is late, so the bars are closing and the wind is blowing down

4

the street, and you hope that if you bike far enough your heart will stop pounding, that your hands will stop shaking.

~

There is a moment when you are alone with your best friend and you want to kiss him but you don't.

~

Every time she tells you that you are weird it feels like someone hammering a stake into your forehead. She is sitting on the edge of your bed and you want to say something honest but instead you find yourself making out again. "I'm spoiled," she says referring to her vibrators. "I'm arrogant," she says, but she has no reason to be.

~

You then realize what you meant when everyone told you that they would never want to read their work aloud, because art talks about truths, the things we are discontent about in our lives and our lovers, and the deeper we get into age and complacency, the less we want to threaten our sex lives, our friendships. We would much rather lie than to be alone.

~

You are sick, you should see a therapist, you are biding your time, trying to eat healthy, trying to exercise, trying to make it to when your healthcare kicks in because you cannot afford to go to the doctor to tell him that your body is failing, that you are failing, that you have given up and everything hurts.

~

There are sometimes moments that don't feel particularly terrible. Like in the morning when you turn on your kettle and listen to music, examine the Christmas lights that are strewn across your table because you haven't yet found a way to hang them up on your wall. You live for the morning moments, because these are the times you feel in control. It takes you 30 minutes to get ready. It takes you 8 minutes to walk to work. Today, you don't have enough money for coffee so you nod at the barista through the window as you walk by. You want a cigarette but you again think about your health. Sometimes it's hard to grab things, to pick things up. This morning you dropped two DayQuil on the floor because your fingers are a little numb. You go through the list of what it could possibly be: stress, malnutrition, cancer, aneurysm, and then you realize you aren't breathing so you exhale and then inhale deeply. You should probably see a doctor. You can't see a doctor.

~

There are moments that don't feel particularly terrible. You call your family every week. Your father worries that you don't take care of yourself (the fear, as it turns out, is well founded). Your mother doesn't really want to know the details of your life because they worry her, so she typically talks about her own life and recounts all the good things that have happened so far this year.

~

There are moments that don't feel particularly terrible. When you bike along the river listening to music, it is always so beautiful that you want to cry, but you can't cry or else it would impair your vision, which could cause you to crash your bike into a pedestrian.

~

There is a moment when you are standing in line, waiting to get into a club (you are not the "going to the club" type, but here you are, in line, with $20 in your pocket and a little drunk). The girl behind you is laughing and falling all over you, the girl in front of you says to you (quietly), "I think she has a crush on you." The falling girl, Parish, has been falling all over you for a while and you know that it will never amount to anything. You shrug and say "I know," and wait in line for two more hours (you don't get into the club).

~

When you go online to WebMD and type in your systems, a pop-up screen comes up that reads "Alert! If you are having an irregular heartbeat, you should contact an emergency healthcare provider immediately!" *I can't afford that shit*, you think to yourself. You close your laptop and think about smoking a cigarette but don't. For, you know,

7

health reasons.

~

There is a time, in college, where you are taking a lot of creative writing classes because you want to write creatively for a living. The classes are fun, often uncomfortable, but that's part of the program. One teacher tells you something that you are unsure what to do with. She says she wants stories, memoirs, essays, that have been fully digested. She doesn't want to hear any stories that are unfolding as we write them. She says this, you think, to discourage writing about college campus hookups, and other school-related drama. You look down your notes. You realize that all you can write about are things that you are currently digesting, things you haven't shitted out yet. You like what a different professor tells you, one year later. "I want stories that are *alive*."

~

There is a moment you are sitting in Hannah's car. You are sitting in the passenger's seat and she is sitting in the driver's seat because you do not drive. And she is listening to you talk about nothing. The correct word is "driveling", she is listening to your "driveling" for almost an hour before you realize she wants you to kiss her, so you do it, reluctantly, and you will yourself to believe that this is great. It is great, you cannot deny this. Her skin is soft and her legs are long so you think "Yeah, this is great, this is great," and you feel like you have disconnected just a little bit from yourself.

~

There is a moment where you wake up and find yourself standing behind an espresso machine. You almost never "wake up" in your own bed. These are the moments where you think, "Whoa, what the fuck am I doing?"

~

You call your parents every weekend. If you call on Saturday, your dad is chipper, he is either on his way to get coffee or has already gotten coffee. If you call your father on a Saturday, you will be tired and you will have work and your voice will be a little bit deep and he will be worried about you. For some reason your mom is not always home; when she is she will tell you a short story about her week and then maybe another story from when you were young, and you will hang up and do laundry. You will do many boring things. You are fine with doing boring things. Sometimes all you want to be is boring.

~

There are moments where you are sitting behind an espresso machine and you will think to yourself "This is where I belong right now, this is exactly how everything is supposed to be."

~

There is a moment you will have the loneliest birthday of

your life. You will be wandering the streets of Portland alone, you will be cold and your back will hurt and you will be carrying a laptop and bundled up clothes and chargers in a camping backpack. You will go into bars too early, you walk the middle part of the sidewalk, the part under awnings which means large, dirty raindrops will fall into your eyes and mouth. Someone will ask you for money and you will ignore them. It is easy to ignore the people who ask you for money. This will change as time goes on.

~

You are performing for friends (you do this often). Performing means practicing semi-rehearsed bits, funny stories for the people that you see during the day. They are all neatly divided into intimacy level and length. You have stories for work, for your barista, for dates (where are these said dates?). You practice them, tell them, refine them, and soon you have a repertoire that you cycle through, and people like listening to the stories and telling them allows you to fill the silence (you are always uncomfortable with silence). There are moments between you and Jan, moments when things are silent, the two of you are sitting at a table together and she is staring at you and you stare back and you think about an article you read that four minutes of prolonged eye contact is one of the scariest and most vulnerable things you can do with someone. You make eye contact with her often because it is easy. When you first began working, you used to make eye contact with everyone. Now it tires you, now too much eye contact makes you feel like a whore. You think of something a friend told you, that scientifically humans have trouble caring about people after they have met about one hundred. You have thousands of Facebook friends. When someone asks you "How many people do you *really* care about?"—you tell them, "Two."

~

There is a moment where you are crying in the snow in front of your college's admissions office, snot running down your face. You are on the phone with your sister who tells you that you should go home. "Or move to Canada," she says, "Brett can get you a job in Canada and you can live there for a couple years." In a couple months you are living at home, back in the Bay Area, hiding bottles of whiskey under your pillow, watching every episode of *It's Always Sunny in Philadelphia* in order. There is a moment where you are smoking and drinking in cars under buckeye trees with friends who talk about all the things they're going to do once they get famous. "Dammit, man," they say, "We oughta be famous already." You are walking down the street with old high school friends who only seem interested in hearing how drunk you get (in honesty, you don't really get that drunk very often). You hate everyone from your high school. You see them in coffee shops and loathe all of them. You drink wine with Kevin and Haley, you drink whiskey with Kevin and Haley, you hit golf balls into the ocean with Kevin and Haley, you eat diner food with Kevin and Haley, you kiss Haley once and never again, you never kiss Kevin though the both of you joke that you probably want to. You smoke blunts in your cousin's garage and he looks at you in the eye and he asks you, "What the fuck are you doing here?"

~

There is a moment that you realize that you might be wrong (you are afraid). When she stares at you and you stare at her back and you freak out over and over again and she patiently waits for it to pass, when you bring her home and talk to her and you want to burn all of your journal entries that contain doubts (you still have doubts). When your writing dissolves, when you are no longer "hard" in the sense that you are angry all the time. There is a moment where she tells you that she wants to go camping with you. There is a moment that you let the word "love" slip out. It happened when you were telling her that three people (including her) posted things on your Facebook wall, "Three people I love," you say, and there is a brief silence. Her hands smell like maple syrup. She claims she farts all the time but you never hear or smell it. "Ninja farting," she says. You are afraid, deathly afraid, of love and caring and loss and appearing weak, you remember when you shook and shouted and cried on the floor of your apartment with Claire, you are afraid it's going to happen again, you have to reorganize your priorities, because you can't do the same things that you usually do every day because now there is another person involved, this person, not your work, must become a priority, this person needs love and attention, just as much as your writing does, and when you are sitting together in coffee shops she reaches across the table, takes your hand and always asks you what you are thinking. "What are you thinking?" This is the hardest question. What you are actually thinking is that you are so fucking afraid, it's hard to pinpoint exactly what, you realize that caring about another person is terrifying because you are not in control, that when you offer your heart to another it is naked.

~

Jan has all these plans. She tells you she wants to go camping, she tells you she wants you to meet her dad. She tells you, "We should do this, we should do that," and you know that all of these *plans* mean nothing until they actually happen (you want them to happen) but you cannot get your hopes up. You are poor, she wants to swing dance, she wants to visit all the cafes you like. There is so much now that the two of you need to *do*, like, how are you going to get around to it all? Will there be room for anything else? Will it be possible to save money? It is possible, but you realize it is the hardest thing. There is a moment where she tells you that you are a "grown ass man," in reference to your apartment and bill-paying ability. Her friends like that. Her friends like you, but you know that friends-of-girlfriends will only like you for as long as she likes you. She is the person you buy gifts for. She is a reason to burn your journals.

~

There is a moment where a friend posts something she wrote on Instagram and it resonates with you. It's a handwritten journal entry that says "My wish for you is that you be who you were before the world broke you." Last night, your friends from church came to see you perform poetry. They sat in the back and left after your performance.

~

At this moment in your life, you reflect and try to identify the people you have truly *loved*. The number you arrive at is three. Hannah, Claire, maybe Jan. Time, you conclude, is the only way you can tell if someone truly loves you, if they stand the test of time, if they are in your life no matter how much time passes, maybe that is what love is. Things are moving relatively quickly with Jan. You are aware that you are consumed by thoughts of this girl and you fear that this will make you boring, you think that when you mention Jan (the all-consuming Jan), that you friends will roll their eyes and tell you to please shut the fuck up.

~

You loved Hannah because she was beautiful and she loved you. You could not believe Hannah loved *you*, for a period of time you were blind to the fact that she wanted you because you couldn't even conceive it to be possible. How many things are like this? Things that we do not see because we do not believe in them?

~

You loved Claire because she loved you more than you can ever imagine, so much that it hurt the two of you, often. You broke up with her because you need physical closeness. Claire did not seem to understand or care about this. You send her e-mails sometimes, she usually responds. The last e-mail she wrote you, she signed it "yours".

~

There are moments when you are writing and think that maybe this time, you will just write this for yourself, that some things don't need to be shared with others, that there is something holy about privacy, a novel written for you and no one else. Maybe this is what you need this year, for you, something that isn't for everyone. You are told often that you need to care about yourself more. "Self-care," it's the buzzword of 2015. You buy yourself Oreos, you gravitate towards people that dish out love because you have so little for yourself. You read an article online where Grace Paley says the key to growing old is to hold your heart in your hands every morning and encourage it. You are trying this, you want to love again, sometimes you aren't sure how your heart is handling it. Maybe it is skipping beats because it is confused. You read Thich Nhat Hanh who tells you that you must make a home in your heart before you invite others in, you liken your heart to your apartment. If you can make a home, a good home, a loving home, you can then share it with others who need it. You want to love in a genuine sense. You are so afraid! Fear is the go-to emotion, is what wraps up your heart; you want to be brave with people, to furnish your heart and invite them to sleep over, to eat your food, and to bring their own furniture, to share your hearts until the world is at home with you. Maybe not the world. You still fucking can't stand certain people.

~

There is a moment when you are at work (you are often at work) Forty hours of your week is at *work*. You enjoy it, you know it is a necessary system you have to partake in. You just got "full-time" at your coffee job, you have a weekend, you are an "adult" And Jan tells you that she can't imagine you ever being *dead* inside. "You are big," she says, "you have a big presence, just like me." You love this. You love dancing around the apartment with Jan. Your bank account will always be empty. How then, you think, will you show her that she means so much to you? You pause, try to reel it back, to remain in control of how you feel, and the problem is that you know that it is impossible. The emotional element of being a human is necessary, even though for so long you thought that being emotional was dumb. It is the opposite of dumb, you think to yourself now. Maybe it is wisdom.

~

There is a moment (in the future) when you will die. It may be (you are worried) from a heart attack. Or maybe you will get hit by a car when you are riding your bike. You might die. You will die. Claire often told you that you "aren't allowed to die." Why? This bothered you the most about the relationship, that she made this impossible rule that you were never allowed to die because of what she wanted. All she wanted was for you to live forever, or perhaps just as long as her. Today, you and Jan talked about your fears. You said you were afraid of 1) household chemicals, and 2) having chocolate on your face. Jan told you that she is afraid, first and foremost, of her family dying. You try to get all philosophical on her, to discuss impermanence, to try and seem smart and disconnected, you tell her that people die, it is a fact of life, and you end by telling her that you haven't lost anyone yet, you aren't even sure what it feels like. Maybe your opinion will change. It is like your friend Brian from back home, who thought he would be okay when his dog died. No big deal, he thought. He was wrong. He was very affected by the death of his dog. It surprised him. Death, you realize, may surprise you. In what it does, when it happens.

~

There are moments you want to cry, when chills run up your spine, but you can't cry, not here, not now, not in front of your barista, not into your hot chocolate. There is a moment when you are walking along the Willamette and you want to sit down and cry because of how beautiful is, how beautiful fall is. The sky is clear and the water is golden blue, and there are wet leaves on the ground. A trio of Segways pass by. You want to cry but you can't. Not here. Not now.

~

There is a moment where you will want to buy gifts for the girl you love. It happened so quickly, you *love* her, you know this but you can't say it (it's too soon). Just a week ago you were bitching about her, saying she was boring, saying she was one-dimensional, you want to burn everything in your journal that says this, no, you love her.

17

You hatch an elaborate plan, you are going to visit her today, unannounced (she probably expects it at this point, she noticed that you have a tendency to show up, unannounced). You can't buy her flowers, that would be too much. Maybe Chinese take-out, you aren't sure, you want to bring her *something* but maybe showing up will be enough. She tells you that she thinks about you all the time. Part of you doesn't believe it. Part of you has to, because you feel you *need* her so much. Fall is coming, and the two of you have made so many *plans*.

~

There is a moment your father asks you "Do you have thoughts of suicide?" You are silent. "You can tell me if you do," he says. This, you think, is how much he loves you. So much that even if you want to die, he wants to know.

~

There is a moment you show up to the movie theater (you are going to treat yourself to a movie), but the movie you want to see doesn't line up with your plans for the day. You called out of work, you are concerned about your heart. Yesterday you ate a burger and it messed with your body-chemistry, you found yourself leaning over your work and being unable to draw a bird. Not even an intricate bird, just one of those shitty birds that look like the McDonald's logo. You went home early and Jan met you at a bus stop, she rubbed your back and listened to you, you feel so *listened to* with Jan, it just drives you crazy.

You think you do a pretty good job of pretending that you don't care too much. Be she tells you it's clear that you like her. And you tell her back that it's clear that she likes you.

~

There is a moment where she introduces you to her friends and you are too drunk to say anything other than "I am really, really drunk right now." You kind of feel bad but there was no avoiding it, the two of you mobbed around on Halloween and ended up in a diner and you kept on repeating "I am really, really drunk right now," and hey, it's the truth. So there's no reason really to feel bad.

~

Claire often tells a story about sitting in the bathroom with you while you throw up into the toilet. "Even when you were blackout drunk, throwing up into the toilet," she tells you, "You were still cracking jokes, you still had a comeback for everything." She tells this story differently now but this is all you hear. All you want to believe is that even when you don't know it, you are awesome to someone.

~

Claire doesn't tell this story, but you know it's true. You are blackout drunk again, in your dorm room, asleep, near death, it appears. You wake up and there is a glass of water on your windowsill (Incredible foresight on your part, you think to yourself). You go to class and open up your notebook and there is a three-page letter from Claire that explains that you texted her while drunk, she showed up to your dorm and pounded on the door. Your housemates let her in, she sat beside your bed and wrote about how much she loves you, she wrote that you look disgusting right now, near death, and she tucked you in and left a glass of water for you, and you woke up not knowing any of this. How many times have people been kind to you and you have been blind to it? How many people have saved your life and then slunk away without saying anything?

~


There is a moment where your friend Brian holds a coin up and tells you "Heads, I live. Tails, I end it all." You immediately try to wrestle the coin from his hands, he tries to toss it but you push it in mid-toss, manage to snatch it as it falls, then pocket it. You want to punch him so badly but you don't. The two of you don't talk about this moment often, the two of you pretend it never happened, but you think about it all the time.

~


There are moments when you walk down the street, listening to music, and you move your arm in the air in a way that reminds you of when you ride the wind with your hand out of the window of a car.

~

Jan tells you that sometimes it seems that you make things dramatic for no reason. You tell her that it might be true, that sometimes you don't feel interesting. She storms away, angry. "Oh my god," she huffs, "You are literally the most interesting person I know. The fact that you even have that worry—" she can't even complete the sentence.

~

There is a moment you realize that one person in a relationship cares more than the other. For the person who cares more, the feelings are more intense, maybe even more poetic, because they have all of this extra angst and yearning for the person that they love. For the receiving end, for the person who cares less, the job is easy. You must always appear to care less, even if things change. Because this is the feeling that the other person is now addicted to: the unrequited love. The forbidden fruit. The yearning. Even if you care, you must grunt and look at your phone and pretend you aren't interested.

~

There are moments where you dance in the morning as you get dressed. Or, to be more accurate, you stop getting dressed to dance. It's sort of hip-hoppy, you hope it looks like you are doing really angular and fresh poppin' and lockin', and in the mirror it looks pretty good. You can't remember the last time you danced alone like this. You've started to do it after Jan mentions that she does this "like all the time".

~

There is a moment you realize that some people are good friends and some people aren't. By "good friends" you mean people who actually want to hang out with you, people who will rearrange their schedules for you, people who will follow through. Robert makes plans and flakes always. So does Robin. You are not a good friend for Heather. You always make plans to hang out with her but then you flake the last minute. It infuriates you when people do this to you, but you find this to be an unfortunate fact about living in Portland: Everyone is too nice to say "no". They will just instead flake on you last minute.

~

There is a moment you walk past a sign that says, "Tree Lighting, 5:30pm, November 27th," and you snap a picture because you want to bring Jan to this. You tell her "I want to take you on coupley-date things because no one has ever wanted to go on coupley date-things with me." This is half true. For some reason you have always found yourself in long-distance relationships which made going out literally impossible. Now that you are spoiled by the presence of Jan, you just want to have this physical nearness all the time. Last night she made you so mad, you were so worried because you didn't compliment her shirt and you thought, "Whelp, this is it, I fucked up." She asked you, "Do you like my shirt?" and you didn't answer right away (it was a pretty basic shirt) and she got mad and went quiet and fixed things around the cafe and you were

22

certain that it was all going to be over, that this was the last straw. But it wasn't. The two of you went out for food and talked about sex and you dropped her off at her house and everything was peachy, peachy keen.

~

There is a moment where you hang up Christmas lights in your apartment. You bought ten feet, which is barely enough to do anything with. You hung it on your wall in a sort of wonky "M" shape and you take a picture and show it to Jan who says, "It looks very *you*." You remember something you read about Beckett. When he taught writing and he didn't necessarily like the piece that a student brought him, he would just tell them that the writing was "so *you*." You know this isn't what Jan meant but you can't push the thought out of your head (you can push the thought out of your head, you do, *but dammit Beckett, why did you have to ruin this moment for me?*).

~

There is a moment when you are sleeping (spooning) in bed with a friend (let's call him Russel) and you reach over to try to hold him, but he flinches, totally freaks out (in his sleep) so you recoil, turn over, and sleep the other way. When you wake up in the morning the both of you pretend it didn't happen. He looks at his phone and leaves.

~

There is a moment when you are fighting with your friend

Ben, you are "slap boxing." There is an open pizza box on the floor and a pile of beer cans (there is no garbage can in the dorm room you are staying in). The game works like this: instead of hitting your opponent, you are trying to slap the top of your head. You move nimbly around the room, trying to slap the top of his head, and it's fun and dangerous, and soon you are out of breath (Ben won, he has hit your head three times). He tells you, "That's the gayest thing I've ever done."

~

*Was college necessarily bad?* you think to yourself. You made friendships that made it possible to fuck around, to do a lot of traveling. You are reading good books and have something of a good work ethic. You conclude that yes, it was worth it, you learned something, you are fine with paying up to $323 a month on student loans (Jesus, that sounds like too much when you write it down). Fortunately you have been able to cut that in half, the amount you have to pay each month, by applying for income-based adjustments, but you are spending all this extra money on Jan, ongoing out to eat, and on medical expenses. As you write this, there is a man to your left who is knocking his fists on the table as he writes, he is shaking his hands and doing strange gestures that translate to "Look at me, look at me, talk to me." Jan did this yesterday. You were reading and she kept on sweeping around you, she moved chairs loudly, she tried to get you to look away from the book and to look at her instead. There is a delicate dance that you are aware of, the one that you try your best to manage. The pretending not to care but being completely clear that you do care. So much of what you read about love is a cultivation of creating a sense of "yearning". Andrew and Robin sit across from you in a bar, and you try to explain to them your fascination with playing games, with teasing the other sex, keeping them guessing. "All I want is a good story," you tell them. Robin nods, looks at Andrew and says, "Yeah, I remember wanting that too. But I think I got over it." This makes you sad, confused, but Andrew and Robin then cuddle close and it seems like they have figured something out that you haven't.

~

There are many moments when you reflect on the beauty of fall. You enjoy wearing gloves. You enjoy walking outside and feeling the wind on your face (hurts your nose). You enjoy walking down the street with Jan as she darts around, breathing heavily, pretending to be a pug. "I feel like I have the energy of a dog sometimes," she says. "Like, I just get so excited and sort of just bounce off walls." She runs and up to a wall and kicks off of it. "Parkour?" you suggest. "Parkour!" she yells, and begins jumping off of trees, fire hydrants. You join her runs circles around her, kiss her at the street corner.

~

You write too much. Michael says that outside of work, all he does is write. He takes his little notebook into bars and drinks, scribbles into his notebook. When you first hang out with him, he rattles off all the cafes and bars that are good for writing. He doesn't go to a certain bar in southeast because they serve coffee in teacups. "I just think that's dumb", he tells you. "If a cafe is serving coffee in teacups, I stop going to it." You often think about the purpose of writing, and the hope is that by writing down your thoughts maybe someone else will feel less alone, maybe you will move someone, change someone, maybe someone will *understand*. You just finished reading a young adult novel, and at the end of the book everyone is unhappy. The genre, you are told, is "realistic fiction". This bothers you, the fact that there is a genre of book that is "realistic", that ends with everyone being unhappy.

~

Every time you bike along the Willamette you experience pure fucking euphoria.

~

You worked at a cafe. You came in, turned on your charm. You realize, now, at 22, that you know how to turn on your charm (it seems to work, people seem to like you). You were so charming and came to the cafe so often that they hired you. This is the same way that you got the job at the library. You volunteered, you turned your charm on, they hired you. Claire tells you, sadly, that she wishes that fewer people loved you. "No matter where you go, people will love you," she says. And you know this makes her sad, because she loves you and she lives across the country and she is aware of how easily you can slip away from her.

~

You take Claire out for her birthday. You take her to a wine bar where you have a nice dinner and you try to tell the waiter that it's Claire's birthday but he clearly doesn't care. Claire is so tense. She is quiet, you realize now that maybe she was just super nervous because she was on a dinner date with you. The meal is mostly silent. You drink wine, she just turned twenty-one, you bring her to a bar across the street and she orders a Sex on the Beach and the bartender doesn't know how to make it. So instead she orders a Kir Royal, which is (from what you understand) champagne with some sort of liqueur added. You take the train back and her friends throw her an elaborate surprise party, they have decorated her room with streamers, there is lots of beer. Her neighbor, Nate, is there. You have met Nate in passing, and he is terrific fun to drink with. You and Nate and Claire sing in the streets, drink a case of beer. Her room is a delightful mess the next morning, strewn with streamers, littered with beer bottles. You run into Nate in the kitchen of the house and he smiles, bleary eyed. "Hey guys," he says.

~

There was a time in high school when you had a crush on a girl named Kai. This is a painful story and you aren't sure why. Perhaps it is because you were in clear denial that she just didn't like you. You were purportedly in love with her. You pined after her, wrote her songs, wrote her poems. Near Christmastime, you duct-taped mistletoe in a doorway and brought her there, she took the duct tape

27

from your hand, taped it over your mouth, and kissed the tape. For some reason you viewed this to be a success. This went on for a while until she started dating something else. Now, you slowly become aware of how much of high school was clouded by denial. Denial about who liked you, who didn't, who were your friends, who loved you.

~

There was a moment you told your friend Jacob that you loved him. "Why can't you just say 'I'm glad we're friends?'" he replied.

~

In therapy, you told your therapist about an elaborate plan you had to take your hot math teacher out on a date. It involved having your friend David drive his car wearing a moustache, pretending to be a chauffeur, because you didn't drive in high school and didn't know how the fuck you were supposed to pick her up and bring her to a Thai restaurant. You spend so much time hatching this plan in your mind that you were legitimately thrown when your therapist scrunched her face up and told you that the idea was weird. *Weird?* you thought, and this made you upset, you thought she would've been super down with the idea. "Why don't you just get a taxi and meet her at the Thai place?" she asked you. You didn't have any money. You couldn't imagine ever having money. You left therapy angry that day.

~

There is a moment where your creative writing teacher looks you in the eyes, narrows them, and tells you that you are a "weird dude." Coming from this professor, this bothers you. The whole semester he has been assigning you the weirdest writing prompts, the strangest essays, and in general trying to push your creative boundaries by encouraging your writing to get weirder and weirder. The fact that he just identified you as "weird" worries you for several years after this moment happens.

~

"Is my nose big?" she asks you, turning over in the bed. "No," you tell her. It's true, you don't think her nose is big at all. "People used to make fun of it all the time," she says. "They used to call me 'witchy'."

~

"Hannah used to cut herself," her brother says. "No, I didn't cut myself," says Hannah, "I just used to poke myself with needles."

~

This is a strange story to tell and you aren't really sure how to tell it. You have tackled it a couple times in your journals, maybe even in this book. This is the time you called your uncle and told him that your family didn't want to see him for Christmas (you were young, you didn't know what you were saying) and then there was a period of time when everyone was freaking out, when your father sat you down and told you "Because of what you said, Uncle James might hurt himself." You stayed in bed for almost a whole day until your dad forced you to get up and to rake the lawn.

~

Sometimes you will sit across from someone over beers and burgers and they will tell you stories that they have rehearsed one hundred times. There are sometimes you will be sharing a meal with this person and you are immediately bored, because they are not telling you anything new, they just need a sounding board for their stories, they just need someone to tell them that they are awesome and worth something. As you pick at your burger and tune out of the conversation, you realize that listening to this man talk about nothing is a little bit like looking into a mirror. In an effort to change the subject, in an effort to try to elicit something real from this person, you bring up heroin, and tell him that you are considering doing heroin (you aren't really considering it, but it's fun to think about), and he is unfazed. The conversation, despite the introduction of (what you think is) the most interesting drug, is still boring. You eat your burger and drink your beer and wonder what you can do to have a meaningful conversation with this person. Maybe it's impossible.

~

There is a moment when you are sitting across from Kevin a cafe. You are writing a novel, he is reading a book. He likes Irvine Welsh and has a fascination with heroin. It is because of Kevin that you think about heroin so much. Grace's boyfriend can't drink anymore because he was an opium addict. Kevin's dad's girlfriend did heroin. It maybe ruined her life. You begin to keep tabs, you pay attention to who has done heroin: celebrities, friends, fictional characters, it doesn't matter. You are just accumulating facts, and you know that it is wrong, that it would ruin your life.

~

There are days you are worried that you are an idiot. When you think that people sort of dance around you because you are socially inept, because maybe you're just dumber than everyone else. Then, there are other days that you feel like Donald-Fucking-Draper. It's hard to figure out which of these realities is true.

~

There is a moment when you buy your friends shots. There is a moment when your friends buy you shots. There is a moment when you are all drunk in front of the bar, huddled close in your rain gear, and you are reading poems aloud together (you have friends).

~

You read an article about Patti Smith (you should probably start listening to Patti Smith, you need to start reading her books as well because her novel, *M Train*, is said to be a masterpiece). You read an article online about all of her favorite books, you think about your own reading list, about all the things that influence *you*. Derrick Brown, Susan Sontag, Woody Allen, William Burroughs, Henry Miller, Anais Nin, these are the literary ones, there are more; Mick Jenkins (it is less rappers and more of their songs that influence you), Mac Miller, Asher Roth. What about the people you hang out with? Ben, Kevin, Jan. What about your ex-lovers? Hannah, Claire? What about your current lovers? You sometimes think that for someone to love you, they must listen to all of your favorite albums, they must read all of your favorite books, they must see all of your favorite movies in order to understand who you are. This is what you do when you spend time with a lover: you tell them that they *must* read this or that they *must* watch that. You have become skeptical about this, it doesn't seem to work. Love, you think, is about sharing new things, watching movies together, developing new connections. It is wrong, you think, to force your past down a lover's throat.

~

"We only take recommendations from the people we love," you tell Claire. "I think that is one of the more true things you have ever said," she tells you.

~

People like your writing. It confuses you. You try to only write the concrete (a man crossed the street, the things you do during the day) in an effort to avoid the fact that you believe nothing. That you have trouble having faith in one thing. You are secretly thrilled whenever someone calls you a psychopath. You tell them, no, you aren't, but you grin, because some part of you just wants to be powerful, manipulative, dominant, and unattached. But then, deep down, there is a child that is crying, there is a tiny, tiny, crippled child that believes it will be alone forever. You look up at Jan, you realize that you may need therapy (what for?). The last time you tried to see a therapist, they told you that you didn't need to see one. Your doctors seem very confident in your ability to live life. You aren't that sure, but their trust emboldens you. You go to church because you feel that God will keep you in check. You feel like being with people who believe in God will teach you how to love. All this as you wash your hands after pissing. All this as you smile and tell cafe customers where the restroom is.

~

You should call your father. There is a moment when you are leaving for college and Hannah is hiding naked in your closet as your father cries and tells him that he is going to miss you. Your flight leaves in six hours. You no longer have a hard on, but you look at Hannah through the slats of your closet as your father is crying in front of you, and for some reason this image stays with you, this image will always be with you.

~

"I like your poem," says Jan. "It's really good." You aren't sure what to think. You don't know how to talk about writing, you feel like you are pedantic, or that once you get going you won't stop. Her friends stare at you funny, disengage when you talk to them. They are uninterested in you, they loll around on Jan's bed and stare off into space. You don't care too much, all you want Jan to know is that you love her (but you cannot tell her that, you cannot say that you love her).

~

Part of writing, you are aware, just feels like torture. Some people tell you that writing is therapeutic. You don't know if these people are right. All you know is that now that you are writing, that you *are a writer*, you cannot stop. You have considered stopping, putting down the pen and saying, "I will never write again, I am just going to focus on living, I will be so much *happier* if I just stop," but you know this isn't true. You get headaches if you go too long without writing. You ache. You get restless. You are in too deep, it is a moment similar, you imagine, to realizing you are an alcoholic. You don't know whether to live with it forever, or to banish it from your life completely.

~

You struggle to think of something beautiful (when you decide this, five painful images pop into your mind: one is sleeping in an empty bathtub, one is you kissing a woman who doesn't love you while you are drunk, one is lying in bed realizing that your uncle may kill himself because you joked that your family didn't want to see him at

Christmas). Then you think of a foggy hill, it is a hill from your hometown. The grass is wet. Your jeans (soft from wear) are wet, your shoes, socks, everything is wet and cold, your feet sink into the hill, the fog is dense, you can see the outlines of rooftops.

~

Sometimes you think that writing is antiquated. Other times you think it is essential. Both times you are too impatient to sit and figure out which one of these statements is actually true.

~

There is a moment when you feel you have exhausted the subject of yourself (it is very similar to the moment when you want to close your laptop and never write again). There is a moment when you squeeze a lemon so hard that there is no juice left, but you keep squeezing and it only hurts your hands. You write about girls, pain, whatever. It feels good, it feels meaningful. You squeeze the lemon. Your hands hurt.

~

You make breakfast, you walk to work, police swarm around a small hobo campground on a street corner. You again feel somewhat alone. You watch *The Nightmare Before Christmas* with Jan, you immediately like the main character because he supposedly "has everything" but is still unhappy. You try to find a specific Nick Flynn poem to show Jan and you can't find it. You wake up to an Instagram photo that Claire has uploaded. You have a nagging fear that Jan will leave you. Most of what you write is a manifestation of worry. You realize your language centers around fear.

~

"I want you to become who you were before the world broke you," Samantha wrote. "I want you to become who you were before the world broke you." You think of when you were a child (either lying in your bed, thinking your uncle was going to kill himself because of you), or you think of when you were a child (when you are standing in wet green grass, staring into fog), or you think of when you were a child (what were you like back then? What broke you? Are you broken?). Your feet sink into the mud.

~

Jan dances around you down the street. "Donuts?" you suggest. She has to wake up early tomorrow, she shakes her head. "I'm trying to change," she says. "With you I've always had this 'fuck it' mentality. I'm trying to do the responsible thing." She wants ice cream but instead goes to bed. You kiss her goodbye. You walk home listening to Green Day.

~

"Have you ever been in love?" Jan asks you. You squint your eyes. "That's a hard question," you say. "I'm not

36

sure." "Then you haven't," she says. "If you were ever in love, you would know for sure. There would be no doubt in your mind." You quietly disagree.

~

Some nights you have dreams that you are catching bullets in your left shoulder. Some nights you have dreams that you are biking off a cliff. Some nights you wake up next to Jan. Most nights you wake up alone. Some nights you sleep like a rock. Constants are few.

~

"Has anyone ever told you you are sexy?" Jan asks you while the two of you are lying next to each other.

~

Jan is shorter than you are, her fingers tapered, small. She has a tendency of laughing too loudly in public places. She likes dancing, she tells you that she has a fantasy where she is the star of a music video. She is wearing something on par with what Britney Spears would wear: lots of straps, very revealing. There is a moment she tosses her hair (she is pretending to be in her music video), and she scrunches up her face into pleasure when she does it, the face singers make when they hit a high note.

~

You are afraid of many things. Are afraid of smothering

the ones you love. The books you carry in your backpack fall apart, because you carry them everywhere. Most of the time you just want to be close to Jan (to someone), sometimes you just need someone to be *there* with you.

~

You see photos of Kevin on Facebook, he takes photos from time to time with his girlfriend. You imagine them fucking sometimes. You are very proud of Kevin and his fucking.

~

"It's like," Jan struggles to find the words, "You do things that are socially unacceptable." You smirk. The delights you. You like the idea that you can get away with things that other people don't.

~

"Hey," Claire massages your back, interrupts a conversation you are having with friends over lunch. "Wanna go?" "Sure," you say. The two of you retreat to her dorm room. She sighs. "I might as well have just told everyone that we were going to fuck," she says.

~

Sometimes you wear the clothes that Claire likes when you miss her. When you wear all black, for some reason it always made her so happy. She would grunt a little, and say, "Black on black. Yes." Today you are wearing black on black. You still have photos of her tucked away somewhere.

~

You are done with pain, you feel like you have sufficiently communicated all of your pain, you wonder if it is possible to write anything different, other than aloneness, pain. Many of your favorite writers express that is difficult to write when they are happy, but you try anyway. Again, you have to think, focus, to identify beautiful moments. There are few. There is one time you were caught in a torrential downpour at school. It came seemingly out of the blue, at the time it felt religious. You attempt to describe this moment but it always falls short. Religious moments so often happen alone. Perhaps this is why they are so hard to express.

~

In the movie *Interstellar*, beings from the future are helping humans find other planets to live on. The only things that seem to travel beyond space and time are gravity and love. Perhaps this is why there is so much friction in good fucking.

~

"I wrote an essay in high-school that a teacher gave me an A on," Jan tells you. "But she pulled me aside later and told me that what was good about the essay was that she could tell that I meant every word, every word had *weight*. Like when you mean what you write, or mean what you say, it has so much more power. It's almost physical." Sometimes you worry that your words don't have any weight. Claire's words had weight. you feel your words are just feathers, you don't know if you believe anything, and because of this you fear that everything you pour onto a page is meaningless. Fluff. A waste of paper.

~

You often think that maybe you should write an "I Believe" essay, like the ones they made you write in high school (you never wrote an essay like this in high school). Your beliefs would be bleak. That humans (including yourself) are easily manipulated. That there is a God. That you love your family. All of these are things you believe but aren't sure if they are true. Everything feels so flimsy, you wish you had something solid to hold, like a body.

# 2
# HORNS

Sometimes it feels like you are walking around downtown with horns sprouting from your head, small little nubs as you light a cigarette and round a corner. You have headphones in your ear, Christmas lights are everywhere, you check your bank account in your smartphone and conclude that you don't have enough money for whiskey. When digging into oneself for material, you come up empty. You write to fill pages rather than to communicate a cause. You have no cause. You only have an odd hurt and a broken love, this limping thing that you carry around with yourself, the thing that you bring to church and pray that Sundays and small groups will fix, that hopefully by going to church, the simple act of showing up and praying, that this will heal you, that this will stop you from going insane.

~

In *The Brothers Karamazov,* someone mentions that prayer is education. Every time you pray, you pray for Chet who lives in New York, Chet who drinks too much, Chet who throws up blood, Chet who has so much trouble saying "No" that it gets him into trouble. One night, you and Chet are sleeping in the same bed, both of you are drunk, and he whispers, "Tell me a secret". You whisper back, "No."

~

You have a strategy for dealing with people. Let them talk. Identify what they want, like. Slowly but surely feed them what they like. Mirror their movements. Rephrase their statements. Let them fill silences. Never give away too much. You are good at manipulating people, you think. You are a good salesman. A friend asks you if manipulation is bad. "Isn't all human interaction just a form of manipulation?" you say. You aren't sure if you believe this, but this is how you justify how you operate. Sometimes you get headaches. Sometimes you are angry. Some parts of you hate selling, some parts of you just want to tell everyone to fuck off, some parts of you just want to point out when people are living their lives wrong. On the bus, Kip tells you this: "I'm more prophetic, you are more pastoral. I hate using churchy terms, but this is the best way I can describe our dynamic. By prophetic I mean that I *talk* about what I believe. And by *pastoral,* I mean that you let your actions speak for you, because you are so afraid of hurting people. You care so much about other people's feelings, you don't want to say anything that would make them hurt. You opt to lead by example." He unwraps a brownie on the bus.

~

The scraping of cream cheese onto a toasted bagel.

~

Milk crusted onto a steam wand in a Berkeley cafe.

~

Jan's waist. The freckles, the moles on Jan's arm, back. The faint smell of syrup on her skin. Her tapered fingers.

~

Dry hands. Rotting garbage. Your toilet hisses. Sunflowers outside your window. Clouds, puddles, rain, fog, homelessness. You ignore the woman who asks you for money.

~

The last drops of hand soap, the last drops of dish soap. The wheezing of an empty container. Urinal cakes. Deep scratches in barroom mirrors. Secrets, things unread, an entire novel that you tuck away for no one ever to read.

~

Over crepes, Jan looks at you. Candle-lit bar. Chocolate

crepe, strawberries. Whipped cream, rain. Disco ball spins small squares of red light around you. You say, "Sometimes I think God gave me this moment, this time in Portland, as a gift. Because things after this may get shitty. I have no way of knowing. But you, Portland, this," you gesture at the crepe in front of you, "these will all be memories that I will have to cling to when God takes this all away from me. He is saying, 'Here is something nice, enjoy it' and I am enjoying it because I understand that my life can get worse. I understand that the comforts I feel are temporary." Everything you love may burn to the ground. "Can I feed you a strawberry?" Jan asks. She stabs one with her fork, puts it in your mouth. You bite a small piece of crepe with the long side of your fork, feed it to her. Somewhere, God groans. The waiter is eating alone in the corner of the bar. Spinning squares of red light. Rain.

~

Catherine moaned your name during sex. So did Jan. You cannot remember if Claire did. Claire told you that she was always afraid of slow sex, of romantic things. "Whenever you look at me in the eyes, it's too much, I have to look away," she says.

~

The screaming in your mind when you make lattes. Your vivid recollections of sex while you quietly tidy things in your workspace. Skin, spit, sex, pussy juice. *Good god*, you shake your head. *I've been reading too much Henry Miller.*

~

"I regret telling you to read Henry Miller," says Ian.

~

Claire said she wanted to pick out your beard hairs with her teeth. She did this only once.

~

Jan does not understand your use of emojis.

~

You wrote "I love Claire" with a sharpie, under one of your wooden chairs. After dating Jan, you drank, crossed it out. You still have Claire's photos. You almost showed them to Jan today as you rifled through your memory box.

~

"The fetishization of secrets," you read in *The Goldfinch*. Words, phrases, images echo in your head. *The fetishization of secrets. The fetishization of secrets.* You want to scream, you want to take a baseball bat to a pumpkin, to something holy, to glass windows. You imagine there is a small gland in your brain pumping out anger, hormones, sex, and you cannot control it, you must destroy things or else this chemical will eat away at your body, you must tear down bridges, you must fuck the steel beams, you jerk off until scabs appear on your penis.

~

Not everything should be beautiful. Brian takes a baseball
bat to his trophies. HE DESTROYS HIS TROPHIES.
They lie in a pile of marble and gold colored plastic. Fuck
the trophies. The two of you drink beers, the two of you
dance on these trophies. You love Brian and his broken
trophies. You love Brian and his dead dog and his broken
trophies. Jan asks you how you are feeling, you feel great,
you do not want to die but you feel like you must always
be ready to die (Jesus, your arrogance, your cockiness, it
knows no bounds). A hot tub shed, a handle of vodka,
drums and bent nails in Brian's garage. Fuck his trophies.
Destroy every trophy you have ever received. Marble dust.

~

Wooden rafters and a hanging stage light. Charlie holds his
hand in his thinning hair, backlit, whiskey. A couple sits to
your left, bent over a lottery machine, moaning. You
loathe every fedora you see. Jan sits to your left, her thigh
pressed against yours, her thigh wrapped in her tights, her
fingers stroke the top of your hand. "Bourbon is God,"
says the man in front of you. People from your church sit
behind you, clean and white with perfectly manicured
eyebrows, fear and righteousness. North Face jackets and
fear. You take a swig of whiskey from a fifth in your
backpack, there is a rock in your brain (these moments you
do not think, it is silly in these moments to even try to
identify what is going on, you have become an animal
again).

~

Your heart falls out of your chest (snapchat). Jan sends
you a photo of her in her bed, wearing the sweater you
loaned her. Makeup is smeared around her eyes. Last night
while walking she tells you that the two of you are so
clingy but are very good at hiding it. You can feel your
bridge creaking. Your heart has never felt this weak.

~

Here's some loathing that comes back to you: the moment
when you are at your going away party and everyone is
there to celebrate your accomplishments. There are hors
d'oeuvres and drinks and family and friends and employers
in the backyard of your home, but you are infatuated,
completely blind to everyone, you are only looking at
Hannah and her legs, you are only touching Hannah and
her legs. You imagine everyone was annoyed at this event,
but you would never know, you did not see anyone. You
were staring at Hannah and she was staring back and
nothing anyone could have said at the party would have
changed anything.

~

It is your last night in the Bay Area, you stand at the edge
of a pier with Daniel. Daniel shakes his head, he tells you
that he will miss you. The two of you are dressed in suits (a
formality for your last day in the Bay Area). The two of
you eat dinner at a fancy restaurant (somewhere neither of

you belong). The color of your ties match. Daniel is the best friend you have ever had. No one else will compare. Because the friends you have through your formative years will know you better than anyone else you will ever meet, after you have perfected the art of outward appearances. You will never again walk with your heart five feet in front of you, you will never have a friend who cries with you at the edge of the ocean, who cries because he may never see you again.

~

"Like the whole night," Daniel says, "you were literally sitting with her on your lap. You were biting her leg. It was disgusting."

~

"So, you and Hannah?" says Isabella. She laughs, you inquire why. "When I mentioned her name, your whole face lit up."

~

Hannah sometimes would collapse onto the floor and wouldn't get up unless you fed her (either food or compliments).

~

Hannah let you drive on the freeway at night, she had you drive her to McDonald's (which was always open), she would buy ice cream and the two of you would drive to somewhere secluded and hump each other there. It was easier to find places to hump in her hometown. Quieter, cleaner, better designed. Her house overlooked the Bay, across the water you could see the hills of your hometown. During the day you would walk to shops with her. She was in control, you were happy to be a follower. With your friends she would watch you with rapt attention as you talked animatedly about the things you were passionate about. She dressed up and accompanied you to shows. Nostalgia, nostalgia. The most beautiful woman you ever dated. Men on the bus ogled at her, looked her up and down, and she huddled close to you (you were almost a head shorter than her) and the staring never stopped.

~

Clean streets, tiny boutiques.

~

Stella is asleep next to you. When she wakes in the morning, she rubs her eyes, tells you that she had a dream about you. "I don't know…" her voice trails off, you believe that is was a dream about fucking. Her father has died, her mother has died. You recommend that she read *A Heartbreaking Work of Staggering Genius*, and she scrunches up her face. "I read the beginning of that, and I couldn't continue, the descriptions of death… the death of his parents, they made me physically sick."

~

Katiana hung herself in a playground down the street from your house. It never got any press. Out of all the things worth reporting about, no one ever read a word about Katiana hanging herself in the playground down the street from your house.

~

Your own mother stays up late and watches reruns of Saturday Night Live, alone. When the rest of the family watches movies together, she retreats to another room, to knit or to watch sit-coms.

# 3

# MONET

Here is something you cannot stop thinking about: you
checked out a book on Monet from the library. It was a
collection of drawings, paintings. Each painting was of the
same cathedral, at different times of day. The whole book
was just the same cathedral, different lighting, different
colors. You love this, it moves you, to draw the same thing
over and over again in the different lights of day. One is
purple and pink. One is blue and yellow. One is clouded
by early morning fog. They are all drawn from the same
angle. Each is exactly the same size. You imagine Monet
dragging his chair out to the same spot in front of the
cathedral every day (perhaps he marked the courtyard with
a knife, perhaps he knew which stones the legs of his chair
should rest on). There are so many paintings, all of the
same thing, all of them radically different. There is no such
thing as monotony, when the lighting of every day is so
different.

~

John Cage just makes you want to hold up a frame to
everything. When you walk to work, sometimes you close
your eyes and listen to the wind between buildings.
Sometimes the smell of piss and rain is comforting.
Sometimes when you walk to work, you can reach your
hands out to either side of you and feel the buildings in the
crooks of your fingers. "There is no such thing as silence,"
said John Cage. Isolated, in a chamber with no sound, he
could still hear his heartbeat, he could hear the electric
hum of his nervous system. As long as there are humans,
there will always be music, and this comforted him.

~

There are moments when you stand behind the espresso
machine at work, hands in your pockets, and you think,
"Just by existing, just by being here, I am helping
someone. My presence, my existence, makes someone else
feel less alone." Jan turned you onto this idea. You find
yourself quoting people all the time. You want to have
your own thoughts, your own original thoughts, but you
are built up of so many quotes, it is like you are hammered
together with them, that you are a spindly monster of
words.

~

You want to hang more art in your apartment. You and
Jan walk around Powell's and look at the ugliest calendars
you have ever seen. You finally find one that is bearable, it

is a collection of paintings of Paris. You have never felt this way before, but you tell Jan that you have this dream, that you want to learn French and go to Paris and learn how to love like the French. It's silly, pornographic, but you've been reading all of these French authors and are convinced that they know a little bit more about love than Americans. It's strictly for academics, you try and convince yourself. But the truth is that you hope it might make you a better lover, it might make you more seductive. "What have you learned, in your reading? About love?" Jan asks you. You think, swirl your beer around. "I've learned that any love, any great love, must be built upon some sort of struggle or obstacle. There must be yearning, there is an element of pain. A *wanting*." "Right," says Jan. *She gets it*, you think, and from that moment on you are convinced she is making things difficult and interesting because the two of you understand that love cannot exist without confusion. Maybe you are wrong. You are always aware that you can be completely wrong.

~

There is a moment when you are reading, alone in your apartment, and you want to cry because you feel at *home*. There is food in the fridge (not a lot, but some). There are decorations on the walls, there are piles of books, there is a bed to call your own. You are so sad, so grateful, that you can't do anything, you crawl into your bed and wrap yourself in sheets, tightly, as tight as you can, to make sure that it is all indeed real.

~

You wake up with a hangover, you have had disturbing dreams in which you were jerking off one of your friends. You have a huge, towering anxiety that you are insane. You spent last night drinking heavily and making collages. You send out a bunch of maudlin text messages (to Jan, to people from college, to Daniel) and you wake up thinking that you maybe should regret the mistakes you made but in conclusion you do not. Claire left a voicemail on your phone. You e-mailed her back during your lunch break, and you are afraid it sounded too lovey-dovey. When you sit and go through your journals with Jan, you can't help but notice how much you write about Claire. "Is this weird for you? For me to look through your journals like this?" asks Jan. The answer is yes, but you say no.

~

Yesterday you felt like crying a lot. This morning you felt angry. Your emotions bounce from one end of the spectrum to another, you try and channel it into art. You worry someone will pick up your art and interpret it as a cry for help. It might be. You used to joke with Kevin that everything the two of you did was a cry for help.

~

You open your heart and empty out the lint. It falls onto your apartment floor. Paper clips, bits of paper, the things that make it hard to breathe. You vacuum it up. You take a paper towel and spray it with Windex, you try to get the dust out of the corners of your heart. You are trying to make your heart a home for Jan, you want to make a little bed, a comfy little sofa, a tea selection, and Wi-Fi, so that when Jan comes over, she will feel at home. This is how you combat your desire to move, to go to Detroit, to tear everything down, to burn everything. You build, you make a nest, a comfy, cozy little home for you to share with weary travelers, the people that you love, the people that you want to be.

~

This morning you cracked open *The Art of War* and skimmed some of the pages, just to see if anything resonated. Who are your enemies? What are you trying to achieve? How are you trying to attain power? You aren't even sure if you are at war, but you feel like you should be.

~

Yesterday you were convinced you were a genius. You stood behind the espresso machine and thought about all the great ideas you had. You saw someone reading a stack of books and thought to yourself, *hell the fuck yes, I could totally write something like that.*

~

You sit in small group, church small group, in the scenic apartment of church friends in Downtown Portland. The small-group leaders are a couple from Georgia, and you love both of them. They are quiet, they listen, they have a 5-year-old son with a trendy haircut who sometimes hugs you and shows you all the cool things you can do on his iPad. He shows you a spider he caught. He shows you his room. He shows you all the things he got for his birthday. When you have girls over your house, sometimes you feel the same way, you just want to show them all the cool things you have. (You did this with Jan, you showed her your journals, your memory boxes. You feel like a child doing this. You suspect it stems from a fear that you, yourself, are not too interesting, but perhaps maybe the things you own *are*).

~

Vincent has a can of berry-flavored sparkling water in front of him. "Whenever I'm sad, or mopey, I put on mariachi music. It's my favorite kind of music, really. Like, when I first start listening to it, it's kind of absurd, but then I can't help but smile, because, I mean, who can frown when they are listening to mariachi music? Here's my idea of what heaven is like: it's Vicodin (or any mild opiate), mariachi music, and a burrito. Like, you can probably do that somewhere in Portland to be honest. I think it is even very possible that there is someone, somewhere, who is doing that right now."

~

You cook with Jan, drink wine, eat breakfast, walk through Christmastime malls, look at jewelry. You have nothing more to say, you are only filled with a quiet gratitude that gathers in your throat.

~

There exists a belief that adults are boring, that old couples don't talk. Perhaps it is because they have shared so much of their life experiences, that silence is a peace of understanding, of knowing, of not having to chat because the both of them *know*. Sure, there is more discovering, but happiness, quiet peace, is sublime. When no more things have to be said, when you reach across the diner table and touch her hand, while she is staring off into the distance, while you are looking out the window, while your cups of coffee become cold.

~

In *Impression, Sunrise* by Claude Monet it almost appears that something is burning. The sun is red, fog (or smoke) clouds our view. There are two (or three) boats, there are people pushing themselves through the water, there are skeletons of ships. Nick Flynn says that teaching poetry is like being the captain of a ship that is moving slowly through fog. Already you feel connected to this painting, *Impression, Sunrise*. You feel ambivalent about its history. You can look online and learn anything about it (it will slip away, we cling to the memories that fuel us), you feel like you are masturbating again (how do you escape this feeling?). You look to God, you look to the painting, you check your phone because you are supposed to get drinks with a friend this evening. *Let me be wrong for a little bit,* you think as a prayer. *Let me learn but give me the freedom to be wrong so that I may love this painting briefly.*

~

Sometimes you feel that you have to tattoo reminders for yourself, on your forearm, like, "I am allowed to make mistakes," a mantra your therapist told you to repeat to yourself, things that you mutter under your breath every morning when you are brushing your teeth.

~

*Impressionism is characterized by somewhat mundane subject matter, creative angles, bright colors.*

~

"Please don't consider me, by any means, an expert in the field," you beg Jan. "But the thing is," she says, "You are more of an expert than I am."

~

What happens when you find yourself to be the captain of a ship that is slowly moving through the fog? It is your job, then, to stand tall for your shipmates, to be unflinching so that they are unflinching. Being a leader, in this sense, is being fearless for your crew, because you love your crew, because at least one of you must bold go through the fog, one of you has to be the one that makes the decisions that no one else can make.

~

You pick at your potatoes, talking to Jan about corporate environments. "I guess," you say, "we have to pick the person who we want to represent us, we need to pick the person who wears the suit." Our leaders. You are afraid of being a leader, but you sense you have to be (a leader of what? A ship moving forward in the fog).

~

In *Impression, Sunrise,* the sun is blood-orange. Red. The sun, and its reflection, are the only red things about the painting, the red light reflects against the fog. Ships appear to be burning. Huddled together in their boats, one person stands to push themselves in a direction (the right direction?). If the passengers of your boat ask you where you are going, you have to believe that you are going home, to safety, to shore. That, or you must make everyone believe that they are going to safety, to shore. If you convince them, this is the greatest gift that you can give to your lost crew, in the midst of dense smoke (fog), in the midst of darkness that chokes them (us).

~

You have a friend (you consider him to be a good friend), who did something simple for you: he would invite you over for soup from time to time. He liked listening to your stories, and he would make you food, expecting nothing in return. You furnish your home, you buy food, in hopes you can be that for someone else, to feed the people you love, to provide a space for them to come when they are crying (kindness breeds more kindness, you think). You will open your home to the ones you love (you realize you do not love everyone, but you try).

~

The phrase "love language" is disgusting to you, you try to think of something better but can't. Your love language is time. Consistency. The way you like showing people that you love them is by being loyal, constant, regular, like a heartbeat.

~

You think, *why do we hate the things we create? Why do we feel that it is not enough?* Perhaps it is because our writing comes short of expressing our feelings, perhaps it is because we feel something authentic and the writing fails to capture it. Writing is a practice, then, in communication. Writing succeeds when you know exactly what the writer is thinking. Maybe. We hate writing because it falls short, it is clumsy, it is an attempt, we make mistakes. You have to love every step of the staircase. You have to look at each step and treat it as your friend. Some of your most memorable moments are the most embarrassing ones. The moments you walk with your heart three-to-five feet in front of you.

~

You are filled with so much doubt. "It seems," you write. "Maybe," you write. "Perhaps," you write. Your feet can't find solid ground in the water. You are standing on the

bow of a ship and reaching your hand through the fog
(you may run into a cliff, you may reach out and feel the
soft leaves of tropical plants). Bravery and courage, it
exhausts you. Sometimes you slump on the gallows of the
ship and reach out your hand. Sometimes you have to
retreat to the cabin and open a small chest that contains
your heart. Just to make sure it is still there.

# 4
# XAVIER

Yesterday, November 13th, 2015, there was a mass shooting, killing, attack, bombing in Paris, France.

~

Yesterday, November 13th, 2015, there was a mass shooting, killing, attack, bombing in Paris France.

~

Yesterday, November 13th, 2015, there was a mass shooting, killing, attack, bombing in Paris, France.

~

Xavier was at the stadium where bombs went off (he is safe, he is safe).

~

Xavier was at the stadium where bombs went off (he is
safe, he is safe).

~

Xavier was at the stadium where bombs went off (he is
safe, he is safe).

~

*Thinking about you,* you text him.
*Hey,* he replies. *Thanks. It's been a crazy night.*

~

Is it wrong that when you kiss Jan, sometimes you think of
him? Is it wrong that when people ask you, "Have you
loved anyone?" the answer is yes. *Who?*

~

You are asleep next to Xavier. You can't close your eyes.
His hands are in front of yours (just grab them). You don't
touch him. You stay wide awake until sunrise. You listen
to your heart, you have to convince yourself that it is
capable of many loves (he has a girlfriend, he knows you
love him). You have written him love letters, you have
asked to kiss him, you think about what it would be like to
be with him.

~

"Do you have sexual tension with all of your male friends?" Jan asks you.

~

"That's a good question."

~

You are in your dorm room with a friend. He looks at you, tells you he has never kissed a girl before, asks you how to do it. "You've kissed a girl before? Right?" he asks. "Yes. Of course I have." "How do you do it? Like, what are the motions?" You think about. "Muah," you say. "What?" "Muah. Like say it with me, 'muah'." "Muah." "That's like a good first step, I think," you tell him. "Your mouth is doing that, it's going 'muah'."

~

"Imagine someone you are in love with," asks your acting professor. You do, you perform the scene, everyone yowls, cat calls. "Who were you thinking of?" they squeal.

~

Xavier is safe with his girlfriend in Paris. Xavier is safe with his girlfriend in Paris. Xavier is safe with his girlfriend in Paris.

~

Xavier is ten (or more) beers in. He has visited you in your hometown. The two of you are standing in a parking lot together, waiting for your ride. "I can't believe I am here with you!" he says. He sleeps at the foot of your bed. A movie plays in front of you, you cannot sleep (Xavier is asleep at the foot of your bed).

~

Yesterday, November 13th, 2015, there was a mass shooting, killing, attack, bombing in Paris, France. The boy you love is there with his girlfriend. He is safe, he is safe, he is safe, he is safe.

~

"Do you think I am gay?" you ask Jan.
"You clearly have something feminine about you. You seem to be really bi, kind of fluid with your sexuality, which I find really attractive."

~

Where do you put all of your secrets? Is there a box, in the cabin of your ship? The box that contains your heart?

~

You imagine Xavier when you are kissing Jan (this is wrong, this is wrong, you don't do this all the time).

~

You and Jan share both of your memories about camping. You tell her about how your father and sister made macaroni and cheese under a tree in the rain (using chocolate milk because that is all that was left).

~

You try to read the articles about Paris, you skim, you try to pick out the information you need. There is so much information, some of it doesn't stick. You skim and see the death count (129) and the wounded count (350), you look at a map of the bomb sites. "Act of War, Act of War," read some of the headlines, big, bold italic. "Act of War, Act of War."

~

You vomit beans and rice on the street in front of your house. You vomit beans and rice into your toilet. Your roommate is passed out by the toilet. You are leaning over a toilet. You are puking into a garbage can. You are staggering home, clubbed to death (it feels) by vodka.

~

You sit on a windowsill and hold a shot of tequila in front of your face. "Sometimes it concerns me, the amount you drink," a friend tells you. You black out, you throw things, you wake up on the floor of Xavier's dorm room. You leave in the early morning, your eyes crusted shut, your mind shriveled and full of pain. Water hurts.

~

*Act of War. Act of War.*

~

You are at home with your family. Your sister is making faces in the window, you are eating chicken and rice and Brussels sprouts. Your father asks your mother, "What was the most interesting part of your day." She will say something nice that happened at work. It is now your turn, you will tell an absurd story, something comic. Your sister will tell of her accomplishments. Your father will talk about something funny that a co-worker said or did. At midnight, you are up late reading or writing, and when you come out for a glass of water or tea, your father is in his underwear, scooping out ice cream from the tub, bleary eyed and half-asleep.

~

You make so many plans with Jan. Camping, restaurants, cafes to visit. The list is laughably long. You do not like talking about plans too much, all the things that you *want* to do with people. You try to always bring yourself back, to the present, to be grateful that Jan is sitting across from you, looking at a shitty painting that is resting on the wall behind you.

~

Monet developed cataracts around 1914, which affected
his sight (you are skimming Monet's Wikipedia page). With
the cataracts, his paintings had a reddish tone. After
several operations, the blues came back. There are theories
that his eyes adapted to the redness, that after the removal
of his cataracts, he was able to see vibrant, ultraviolet
wavelengths. He repainted certain paintings during this
time, you can see the differences in his perception of color.
The same image at different times. The same image with
different eyes. The same image at different times of day.

~

The more you write, the more you are interested in the
exact definitions of words. "Define Impressionism," you
Google. "A style of painting originating in France," you
read, "characterized with a concern for depicting the visual
impression of the moment, especially in the terms of the
shifting effect of light and color."

~

Portland is grey today (you love fall, you walk through
Pioneer square and imagine the Christmas tree that will be
here soon). The trees are covered in lights. You and Jan
walk through Macy's together. She browses shoes, jewelry.
Red, gold, cold, grey.

~

"Sometimes, you just need a place to be broken," says a friend at your church small group. "No one has it together."

~

Sometimes you want to hold kaleidoscope up to the bridges of Portland against the overcast sky so that it looks like a spider web of steel. Sometimes you just want to tell Jan, "I love you," but you feel it's too soon. You always want to call her sunshine but aren't sure if it's appropriate. She is your sunshine (you begin to sing in your head). *Sunshine, sunshine.*

~

Today it is cloudy in Portland. Overcast, cold and wet. *Sunshine, sunshine,* you think. You feel silly about it, all of your lovey thoughts. When you kiss her in the street you imagine that someone is always about to say "Get a room!". *You can be in control, be in control,* you think to yourself, and your heart flutters, you feel a sob rise and catch in your chest. Sometimes Jan curls up into a ball in your bed and you wrap her in blankets. Sometimes you curl into a ball and she wraps you up. "Little burrito," she says, and your stomach flips, because of how many times you and Claire talked about "burrito-ing" each other in sheets.

~

Varying light. Different eyes. Different times of day.

~

You brush your teeth and go through basic hygiene and maintenance tasks. You clean your kitchen sink, but not often enough. You fold all your sheets, you make your bed. You play some soft rap music, you bend over to check the status of your garbage can and conclude you can go a couple more days without emptying it. Why, do you think, do you feel this growing love in your head? This heavy, full gratitude that adds meaning to each of these mundane, morning tasks? What happened to the sarcasm you loved so much? What happened to the cold, brittle distance, the harsh laughter? You are aware that you probably haven't found an answer, any answer, as to how to live or how to be happy, but this love (that seemingly comes from nowhere) fills your heart as you bend down to pick up a small zip tie, as you use a Swiffer to gather up all the pubic hair that has accumulated in your kitchen.

~

You doodle for an hour and show your friend what you drew. It's supposed to be abstract, you wanted it to be something that looks mechanical (it has pistons, gears, some steam-punk aspects to it). You wrote words, you shaded it, you made sure that you "filled the space." And you show your friend and he squints his eyes and says, "Dude, you literally just drew a massive cock. Look at it. It's clearly a dick."

~

*Impression, Sunrise* is one of six paintings of the same harbor in Monet's hometown.

~

Yellow, hill, grass, fences, decay, river, mud, swing, beige, boxes, hoodies, bicycle, 2003, Trader Joe's, bump, hype, Dorito bags, yell, squeak, tile.

~

"You should never share this book with anyone," Jan tells you. "It sounds meditative. Self-exploration, you know? You should just keep it to yourself."

~

You go through your iPhone notes, you find that quote by Marianne Williamson, "Our deepest fear is not that we are inadequate. Our deepest fear is that we are powerful beyond measure."

~

Deluded. Delusional, half. Half. Emphasis on half. You fill the void with a shot of whiskey, you fill the void with God, you fill the void with anything that fits, like a child frantically going through blocks, trying to find the right piece for the hole in his heart. You are maudlin, you are critical of yourself, you are trying to shine but looking for the places light can pass through.

~

There is a moment where you are convinced she does not love you. There is a moment you will try to protect your heart (you read over and over again that trying to reason with the heart yields no results). You read over and over again that you are worth something, that you can shine despite your flaws (imagine yourself in a basement, holding a flashlight at pages, trying to find something that will save you).

~

Some of the things you read are terrible.

~

Some of the things you read are ambivalent, flat. They say nothing. They have no fire.

~

You hurt (everyone hurts).

~

You happen to be in love (hopelessly) with Xavier. Perhaps, if you write some sort of fantasy, a romance, a novel, that expresses this truth, it will feel real enough. Perhaps you can write a novel in which you and Xavier somehow overcome the distance and his girlfriend and all the opportunities you let slip through your fingers. You take great gambles, but seldom with love. Where is your heart? It seems you have misplaced it.

~

Cartwheels. You read Jan some of *I'll Give You the Sun* by Jandy Nelson. "This is inappropriate," she remarks. "This is just erotica." "But there's no sex," you tell her. "But it reads like erotica."

~

You cannot imagine ever being completely sober, like as a rule, like in a program. The thought of never having a drink again is terrible, it is like the idea that you will never love wholly and fully again.

~

You check your e-mail for messages from Claire. There are none.

~

"No one wants to read your thoughts," says a stupid little voice in your brain. You find this funny, because Jan, Claire, Hannah, all they ever told you was, "I want to know what you're thinking."

~

Hurt. Every hurt. A small line of hurt waiting for a bowl of soup. A line of hurt in the snow waiting for a bowl of soup. You are the one serving the soup.

~

*Say what you mean, speak plain.*

~

The bravery, the drive, to write something truly terrible. All of your doubt, gathered in one place, for people to nail up onto a wall for everyone to ridicule. *Here I am, here is all of me,* you look up and listen and hear nothing.

~

Five people this week have bought your book on Etsy.

~

Kindergarten: I want to be an artist. Second grade: I want to be a writer. Sixth grade: I want to be a movie director. Twelfth grade: I want die. As soon as possible.

~

Something happened.

~

Here is your heart. It is tied to a string that is tied to a boat that is leaving shore. The problem is that it is still your heart, and as the boat moves, it pulls the string that pulls your heart, and (in theory) pulls you, unless you let it go, unless you become a shell on this island, if you do not tell Xavier that you still love him.

~

Your love for Xavier is a lie, you tell yourself. You shake your head. How many fucking times can you say this? How well do you even know Xavier? Why are you beating yourself up about this? Is there any way you can let this go? You have given it so much energy, so much attention, you have done everything you can? He knows, for chrissakes. He knows that you love him, you cannot change any of this. Let go, let go, let go. the ship is departing (is it taking your heart?). The ship is departing and you are trying to reason with the steel.

~

Your hands hover over the keyboard (*How do you get over someone?*). By focusing on yourself. By repairing yourself. By building your own ship and becoming captain of it. You have been sailing and sinking. It is time for a new boat.

~

In *Impression, Sunrise*, the sun is the same brightness as the rest of the painting. If you turn the painting black-and-white (that is, if you alter it with a computer to strip it of its color, or if you print it on a black-and-white printer), the sun will be missing, it will be indistinguishable from the sky. It reminds you of the sky in Portland, where you cannot see the sun that often anyway.

~

The vacuum in your heart (this is what Thich Nhat Hanh calls it). You will fill it with art, you resolve. You will fill it with whiskey. Or, perhaps, seal the broken holes.

~

"What is bad for the heart is good for art," says a character in *I'll Give You the Sun*. Something like that. You are skeptical. The heart seems to go through so much, you are surprised it's still up for the challenge sometimes.

~

When you are wavering, you ask yourself, "What is inside my control? What is outside my control?" You breathe, you try to self-medicate (in a stitching-back-together sense).

~

She is asleep, alone. You are asleep, alone.

~

You are not in a bicycle gang, but in the morning as you

get your coffee, you sit and watch an actual bicycle gang get ready, you watch them drink coffee and smoke cigarettes and speak into walkie-talkies strapped to their shoulders. They are grungy-looking, caked with dirt and tattoos and none of them wear helmets, at least the times that you've noticed them.

~

Last night the hole in your heart, you tried everything to stop the leaking. You filled it with hot chocolate, you filled it with photography books, you filled it with Monet, you filled it with quinoa, but the only thing that seemed to work was filling it with a phone call from your sister.

~

Last night you opened up the Bible to "Psalms," hoping it would fill the hole in your heart. It didn't. *This was a mistake,* you think. *Writing about yourself. You should've done something else, like write a fiction about biker gangs.*

~

You have a hole in your jeans. You want to sew it up, patch it up somehow, but you aren't sure how that works. All you want to do is stop writing. All this month, plus a couple times this year you think, "I should stop, writing isn't good for me," but you can't stop, it'd be silly to stop, it's so much of your identity. Is it bad? Does it matter? You are digging graves for everyone, you are digging a grave for yourself, you are bleeding yourself into a well.

~

Perhaps this is the halfway point. Perhaps you can switch it up here. Perhaps you can go in a completely new direction, because the self-analysis, the self-flagellation, the digging, it is digging a hole to the other side of you. *Less of this, less of this*, you beg. Burroughs says the writing comes because there is no other option. You have other options, sure (debatable). You write such shitty, terrible things about other people. Where is the love that filled your heart just days ago? What happened what happened what happened? A chemical imbalance? A lack of knowledge? If you read a book, if you went on a jog, if you were madly in love, isn't that the goal, wouldn't all the existential bullshit go away if you simply learned to stop thinking? To turn off the radio noise, to turn off the doubt and to quietly shine like a night-light, like Christmas lights, like a Jack-o-Lantern? *I am here for you,* you think, closing your eyes and clenching your fists, not sure exactly who you are aiming the thought at, but maybe if you clench your fists tight enough, the light will shine out of your ears and eyes and asshole and pores. Maybe you will explode (you won't). Maybe you will feel better if you just shine like this, instead of wondering why you are empty (it is for the light, you have to make space in the heart for the candle or the lightbulb, whatever you choose to put in the cookie-cutter hole in your heart).

~

You can't switch it up here. What the fuck man. Are you serious? You're halfway through. Might as well keep going.

78

~

Caffeine abuse. Caffeine doesn't make you a genius. Caffeine makes you *feel* like a genius. Which, sometimes, is enough.

~

"Do you want to get your palm read?" Jan points over to a tent where a woman is hunched over a pile of tarot cards. "No," you say, "I'm not ready." "They're like self-fulfilling, aren't they? I feel like getting a palm-reading is a commitment in that sense, that just by the act of getting your palm read, you start making a prophecy for yourself."

~

Last night you couldn't sleep again. You wrote a shopping list: sugar, honey, cookies. You made yourself hot chocolate, splayed some books across your table, studied books on shoes and sex, Monet, mech drawings. You don't know what you are looking for, you are trying to poem, you are trying to find something, you are trying to fill your heart with something to pour out.

~

*You can't pour from an empty cup,* says a friend from church. You have never heard this phrase before. They explain it to you. You cannot care for another, you cannot love another, unless there is already love inside of you. *You can't pour from an empty cup.*

~

*There are many things of which a wise man might wish to be ignorant,* wrote Emerson.

~

You lost your second pack of cigarettes (it's a sign). You want to buy a third, the allure of cigarettes (*kill me, please, quickly*) is almost too much to handle, *why not why not why not.*

~

Why did an 8-ounce coffee feel like it wasn't enough (your tiny body usually can't take more than eight ounces, tonight you are roaring, you are not a genius yet). *8 ounces 8 ounces 8 ounces.*

~

"Do you want a hit of this weed?" asks your co-worker. You take the pipe, his lighter. The wind is too much, you don't smoke weed, it doesn't light. Your co-worker watches you, deadpan. Shrugs, takes his pipe back. "That's too bad."

~

"What do you look for when you check out a woman?"

"Wrists, ankles, legs."

She thinks. "In men, I'm into like, the slim man hips. You know how a woman's hips are wide? I see a man with narrow hips and I'm really into that." You know that some women are into veiny forearms. Sometimes you will flex your forearms, try to see how veiny they are (they're pretty veiny). *Fuck yeah, veiny forearms.* You clench, unclench, massage the sinew.

# 5
# THE SICILIAN BULL

The Brazen bull, or the Sicilian bull, is a torture device, Vincent tells you. The bull is hollow, made of bronze, and a person is placed inside. A fire is lit beneath the belly of the bull, and the person is cooked alive. His screams are muted, and come out the bull's mouth as the sound of a whistle or just the sounds of a bull's grunts. "It's more mythological than historical, I think," says Vincent. "The idea is that a tortured man's screams can come out of the bull as a song."

~

In *The Pillowman*, the writer's brother is tortured in the next room. The purpose is to give the writer nightmares, to improve his writing.

~

William Burroughs is often quoted to have said he didn't know how to really write until he accidentally killed his wife (he shot her in the head).

~

Writers, comedians, they are widely consumed, so many of them are sad. So many of them kill themselves. So many of them cannot be anything other than what they are.

~

You are full of all these *facts*. These tidbits of information that somehow make your life livable, that somehow give your life some context, that somehow give you permission to do whatever you want, so you can say, "Well so-and-so did it, so I guess I can do it too". *Who are you? Who are you? Who are you?*

~

You are at the top of a well (at the surface), you are yelling into it "Who are you?" and it echoes back "Who are you?" You try again, you yell louder, "WHO ARE YOU?", so hard that it hurts your throat, you yell so long and hard that it reverberates down the well, it comes back only as a hum (the Sicilian Bull).

~

You walk a block, pretending your right foot is deformed, curved inward. You limp your way down a city block, just to see what it feels like. You tell Jan this. "That's weird," she says. *OF COURSE IT'S FUCKING WEIRD THAT'S THE POINT,* you have no patience for people who shy away from the weird. *Give it to me, give me all your weird, drown me in it, tie me to a bed and strangle me with it.*

~

Your creative writing teacher narrows his eyes. "You're a weird dude," he says.

~

A potential employer looks you up and down, her eyes linger on the aluminum baseball bat protruding from your backpack. "You look like a psychopath."

~

"Breaking up is hard," a professor says. "Who here likes breaking up with their significant other?" You raise your hand, people laugh. The professor laughs. "Well, you have issues," he says.

~

"You're cracking up dude," your sister writes you.

~

You are looking for beautiful things, you are checking under your bed, you are cleaning your dishes, you are sitting in your chair, eating a bowl of oatmeal, staring at your Christmas tree. Your bike sits out in the rain. This morning you dance around with Jan, last night she told you she wanted to be your girlfriend. You feel anxiety in your chest. So much of this scares you. You pretend not to care, you pretend not to care.

~

You have a morning anxiety. You try to take deep breaths, they catch in your throat, you cannot fill your lungs all the way (frayed ends).

~

You show Jan some poems that Claire wrote. "I'm kind of jealous. I feel weird because you like her poems. I feel jealous because you think she is a talented poet."

~

You want to run forever. You want to pull off some Forest Gump type bullshit and run into the middle of the desert. You want to sit back on the hood of your car in the middle of the desert like Steve Jobs and drop acid. You want to do coke, last night Jan freaks out when she learns you have never done coke. You have stories to tell Jan, you just talk at her, you try to listen, you think you are doing a good job. The dancing, the fine line, the thought of her leaving you.

~

Your apartment is messy. On Monday nights you go out with Jan, on Tuesday mornings you get coffee. You like the rhythm, you appreciate constants, you worry that relaxing, that settling in this routine, will destroy romance between you and Jan. Anxiety peaks.

~

You left ramen out all night (it's probably okay, it's a lot of food, it's gonna have to be okay).

~

Around Jan, you just throw money around like it's nothing.

~

You sit across from Jan in a bar with your friends and you are aware that you are probably being really, really coupley, you fear that it annoys your friend Robert, he leaves with his friends.

~

"I dreamt that you were writing things on soup can lids," whispers Jan with her eyes closed.

~

There is a moment when you will wake up and look away from Jan (sometimes you find it is hard to look at her, sometimes she angers you, sometimes she disappoints you), you look away because you want to yell at her but you don't. Full of self-doubt. Full of thoughts. You kneel by a river and try to let them go. You furrow your eyebrows and think about all the Thich Nhat Hanh you've read. He says that if you pour salt in a cup, it becomes undrinkable. If you pour salt in a river, no one notices. The river is love, he says.

~

"I like the idea of long distance relationships," says Claire. "Like, what are the odds that your soul mate lives down the street from you?"

~

"Fate makes no mistakes," Hannah used to tell you. The two of you put up stickers around town, whispers beneath bridges, "Fate makes no mistakes."

~

"You aren't allowed to die," Claire told you.

~

Last night, Jan looks you in the eyes and says "Nothing is allowed to happen to you." Why does this always happen, why have both Claire and Jan made this rule, that you are not allowed to die, to become injured, to be taken away from them. "No," they say, they trace a circle around you, they draw in the sand a small halo of protection. "Don't leave, don't die."

~

You often think about orbits. Imagine yourself as a planet, moving in an ellipse around the sun. Imagine your orbit of coffee shops, work, interests, the things you revisit over and over again. You see the full moon monthly. You see a meteor shower perhaps once a year. Haley's comet orbits the sun every 75-76 years. When, you think, will you run into your soul mate, your other half? Are they in your orbit or on the other side of the moon?

~

"I reject grooves," Tim tells you. "I am the scratch in the record." He is a spaceship in this sense, the line that intersects the orbits, that transverses the planes.

~

You bike down empty, wet streets, blasting music in your headphones, bobbing and weaving, mouthing lyrics. Lights on the water, lights on the bridges, tight corners. You imagine you have bat wings. You imagine you are one of twelve. You imagine (as you bike across the bridge) that you careen over the edge. You would position yourself correctly, you would not gasp when you hit the water (if your legs break, you would scream bloody murder). The last thing you told Jan was that you were going out to be a "night monster." "What does that mean?" she texts you.

~

There is a moment you will shit yourself on the way to work. You will be walking down the hall of your apartment and you will fart. A little nugget of shit will fall out and you will waddle back down the hall, shower, clean your boxers, then curl up in your bed for an hour (you will wonder how on Earth you will muster up the courage to go to work). Somehow, you find yourself there an hour later, smiling and sitting across your friend Ryan who tells you that his mother is so paranoid that she carries around a little emergency kit in case she ever shits in her pants.

~

There are one hundred ways you can die. There are one hundred ways your relationship with Jan can end. She tells you that she was talking to her friends over Skype, she told them, "I think I have a boyfriend." No one has ever (sincerely) called you their boyfriend. You tell Jan this. It's a big deal. You try and pretend it's not a big deal. For chrissakes you are twenty-two years old. And the girl you are dating happily calls you her boyfriend. At work a co-worker approaches you. "You have a girlfriend!" she squeals. You smile. "I do!" She is asleep, asleep, asleep (she is always asleep when you are awake). You pull sheets around her, bundle her up, contain her with your arms, your chest, your body (you are her cocoon). She can be asleep like this, and you will be her outer shell.

~

She holds her heart three feet in front of herself. She tells you the truth and sometimes it sends you in circles. When she can't hang out, she can't hang out. You want to believe it's something different (another man, or she hates you), but she is being sincere. She holds her heart three feet in front of her.

~

You are in elementary school and you have been wearing your pants backwards for half of the day. You hadn't noticed until this moment, the moment you try to put your hands in your pockets and you can't because they are facing the wrong direction.

~

You examine all your blemishes (red marks on your face, redness on your arms, zits, cuts). Your immediate reaction is that you want to go to the doctor. Your second reaction is to wait two days. Waiting two days, eating some vegetables, drinking water, all of this heals you.

~

You sit across the table from Ryan who writes on tiny pieces of stationery. A man behind him is turning napkins into flowers, a woman behind you is fighting with someone over the phone, two men to your right are playing Go.

~

You have trouble walking in a straight line sometimes. You don't drink enough water. You are convinced that you are going to accidentally poison yourself when you cook in your own house.

~

You fear returning to your apartment and seeing it has burned to the ground.

~

Part of you understands that Jan might leave you (you love her, you love her). You encase her in your sheets, you hold her fingers.

~

Sometimes you think you are better at writing music than you are at writing novels. Sometimes you wish you can just turn all the things you write into songs, maybe then they can slide into your ear a little easier, maybe then you can enjoy singing them.

~

There is a moment when you will stare at yourself in the mirror and dance (you dance so much more now, you dance around Jan in the morning). You spend all of your money on Jan (it doesn't feel like spending money). You most likely look a fool. You don't care. Many fools don't seem to care that they look like fools.

~

You are consumed by lies.

~

You thrive on lies.

~

You drivel about nothing.

~

Here you are, in the white Prius again, driveling for hours, talking to Hannah who is waiting for you to kiss her.

~

"I think you are just a nice person who tries his hardest to be an asshole," Maya says before she kisses you. *Where are you?* Claire texts.

~

You want to rip your face open, spill out all the change into the sink.

~

You want to rip your heart open and fill it with
secondhand furniture.

~

You want to rip your brain open and take a huge shit in it.

~

You are (instead of full of shit) full of ginger tea.

~

You squat down to examine the growing sprout. You
squat down to examine the growing sprout. You feel like
an alien (you are looking at the sprout from all the wrong
angles).

~

There is a moment when you will build an ark (similar to
Noah's), and instead of an ark it is a book and instead of a
flood it is a car accident.

~

Rain (in Portland). It came back. You jump around
puddles, Jan stomps through them. You buy her some
beers, she touches your leg. You are obsessed with her
every movement, how can you write about anything else,
when you find her to be the most interesting part about

you.

~

Your friend writes you a letter of recommendation for a job, says that you are "often surprised" when someone tells you that you have done a good job.

~

You get drunk in your apartment and make collages. You blast rap music and "make art."

~

You buy cigarettes because you can't walk straight (you don't drink enough water).

~

*Where*, you frantically check your jacket pockets, *where are the whole parts of me? Where are the things I can be proud of?*

~

You are up late. On Facebook. You only look at your own profile. You only look at your own Instagram. You count the likes, you look at who *likes* you. You keep tabs on the people that seem to *like* what you post. You check all the time after you post things, you thirst and hunger for the likes, it feels like what you are doing is worth something.

~

Writing as something holy (*a rite*, says Thich Nhat Hanh).
You regulate your breathing (the holiness of late-night
cafes, the holiness of midnight breakfast food, the holiness
of your sleeping lover). *Where is she where is she where is she.*
Asleep, alone, beneath her halo of Christmas lights (your
angel). The angel stands on the precipice. The angel turns
sadly to look at you, in a way that tells you that the angel
belongs to no one (with that, she burns, she falls).

~

There is a moment when you are camping (your hands
have sap between the fingers, your socks are thick and
woolen). You and Hannah fumble around in the tent,
hooking up, touching each other, while the rest of the
family is out hiking. The sounds of flapping fabric, the
rustling of sleeping bags, the static in your hair and the
shocks of electricity between your two bodies.

~

You wake up to a phone call from your father, who checks
in with you weekly. You go to a diner down the street and
empty some ketchup onto your plate, and accidentally on
your smartphone as well. You bike with Jan to her job in
Southeast Portland, and try your hardest to act normal
when you talk to her co-workers. There is a delicate
balancing act that occurs when your friends meet your
other friends, or when your significant other interacts with
an acquaintance. Your strategy is to remain quiet, assess

what everyone knows about you, before entering the conversation. You play up to everyone's image of you, you make sure you become a combination of everyone's expectations (God forbid you ever act like *yourself*).

~

Outside of a midnight cafe, a man chain-smokes Camels and paces back and forth, discusses body alignment. His shoes are a black plastic, his hood has fur around the edges. He paces, comes inside for a black coffee, returns outside. He's been on the phone for an hour, maybe two. When you come outside for a cigarette, he has set up a small boombox and is blasting techno music. You check your phone, it is 1:00 a.m. in the morning and no one seems to care. Inside the cafe, the barista plays with a long tuft of hair behind his ear and sings along (softly) to the music playing behind the counter. A pear-shaped man flirts with the pear-shaped woman behind the espresso machine, a couple on the couch observes everyone quietly with concerned looks on their faces. You don't have headphones. You order ginger tea and try to write (the writing goes well), when you start to nod off, you come outside again for a cigarette and the man in the shiny black shoes is still pacing about, discussing how, "she needs to be more spiritually open".

~

You finally cave, you tell Vincent about the dream you had, the one where you were crying and jerking him off. He laughs, the both of you laugh, the both of you laugh hard and can't stop.

~

You are drenched, your cigarettes are soggy from biking through twenty minutes of mist.

~

Every morning you leave your apartment and fear that when you return, it will have burned to the ground. Every morning you leave your apartment you check once, twice, sometimes a third time to make sure everything is off, to make sure that all of the stove burners are cold, that your Christmas lights are unplugged. Every ambulance and police car that drives by, every siren, you assume it is people rushing to your apartment building to put out the flames.

~

"Eight years," Vincent tells you. "I've been together with my girlfriend for eight years. It's a good story, one day I'll tell it to you."

~

Rain in Portland, Rain in Portland. Your hands are warm when you peel off your gloves.

~

You sit and read Thich Nhat Hanh in front of Ryan, who scribbles on tiny, tiny stationery.

~

Here is a painful memory: It is your last night in the Bay Area, you are ignoring your best friend and instead biting Hannah's leg.

~

Everything comes one hundred miles an hour, like rapid fire (you sometimes have dreams that you are catching bullets in your left arm).

~

You want to take her eye contact (her attention), distill it, inject it directly into your veins.

~

She sits across from you, looks at you as she drinks her coffee (what if you are blind, what if none of this is what you are actually seeing?). Love too often makes one foolish, blind. Last night, at your job, you prayed (as usual) for the safety and health of your friends, however, for the first time (in a while), you also prayed for guidance. *This is new*, you thought to yourself. *Dear God, please guide me. Dear God, who knows me much more than I know myself.* People walk past you, ignore you, walk away with their lattes.

~

There is a moment when you are sitting next to Lindsay, smoking cigarettes as your campers sleep. You checked out *The Oxford Book of Prayers* and are carrying it with you, just because you fear that you aren't interesting enough to hold a conversation (you can read a passage from the book perhaps, maybe she will be interested). "What's that?" she asks. You show her. "Are you religious?" she asks. You shake your head, "No". You light cigarettes. Your campers are supposedly asleep.

~

You smoke cigarettes because you once read that Native Americans believed that their prayers were carried to the heavens by tobacco smoke.

~

*Dear God, be good to me. The sea is so wide, and my boat so small.* This is a prayer that you cannot get out of your head, this is the prayer that echoes in your quiet hours. *Dear God, be good to me. The sea is so wide, and my boat so small.*

~

*I'm allowed to make mistakes, I'm allowed to make mistakes, I'm allowed to make mistakes.*

~

You are in a tunnel beneath the freeway with Daniel. When you sing, when you yell, the sounds reverberate, echo so that the entire length of the tunnel hums. You and Daniel make up Gregorian chants. The two of you hop puddles, take photos, smoke weed on the ledge.

~

You are in the tunnel beneath the freeway with your friend Liam. He has spray paint, you made stencils. You make your mark, you are afraid of all the toxins in the spray paint. You hold your breath, and walk away to breath.

~

You haunt, you haunt, you haunt (repeat in threes).

~

*I'm allowed to make mistakes, I'm allowed to make mistakes, I'm allowed to make mistakes.*

~

Sometimes at work, you will remember something stupid you've done. You will mutter "fuck" under your breath, then look up, terrified, worried that someone had heard you.

~

You are always thinking about your exit strategies. You

always want to burn everything to the ground. With Jan, you have no exit strategy. You can't bring yourself to even fathom one.

~

You inject her eye contact into the biggest vein you can find (you slap the veins to that they rise to the surface, you clench your fist and tie a tourniquet around your bicep). *Stare at me forever*, you think as you wrench the belt tighter with your teeth.

~

*How many times has Detroit burned?* You make a mental note. You need to open up your books on Detroit and identify all of the major ones (all of the minor ones). Every time a house catches fire. Every time something (like a blood vessel) ruptures in your heart.

~

Kelly has pink bags under her eyes. She works full time, is going to grad school. She is a poet. "I've seen some really bad open mics at PSU," she says. Her eyes are heavy. "Lots of poems about ribcages." She chuckles, catches my eye. "You know what I'm talking about, I'm sure. "

~

You gulp coffee and immediately think, *you shouldn't drink coffee like that, like it's water.* You don't drink enough water.

You get dizzy, you go to the hospital one too many times because you don't drink enough water (hopefully your cigarettes aren't wet, you need to send a prayer soon).

~

"Sometimes, I feel like I'm retarded. Just because of all the drugs I've done," Beatrice tells you as the two of you watch the sunset.

~

Hold your heart in your hands, tell it something encouraging. *Your boat is so small,* you whisper. You hammer together your ark. The sea of floating corpses. There aren't even any seagulls left to pick apart the bodies. This is a lie. There are two seagulls, lazily flying above the ruin, you wonder if they will ever notice what's happening beneath them.

~

Your heart rate increases, you drank the coffee too fast. Abuse. Abuse. What happened to the language that cared so much? Where is this river of love that Thich Nhat Hanh speaks of? "Has Thich Nhat Hanh ever been in a relationship?" Vincent asks you. "Be wary of the advice you take from celibate monks."

~

*I hold back,* you tell Jan. *Why?* she whispers back. You tell

Vincent that it is because you are protecting your heart.

~

It is so hard to keep track of the characters in your life.

~

Just tweets. You want to dig deeper, you want to create something cohesive and whole but you think in bullet points, sentences, small bursts of bullets (perhaps the ones you are always catching in your left shoulder).

~

You cannot sleep, you think there is something beautiful in insomnia (it has to do with aloneness). You woke up at 4:00 a.m. with a hangover, realized that you spent the night drinking a combination of sake, whiskey, and beer. In waves, it all comes back (as you wobble over to the sink, get yourself a glass of water for the headache). The night started at Ryan's house, where he made you soup and you listened to Portland chefs discuss what they should make for art openings. "Let me show you the stripper pole," says Ryan, who takes you up to his bedroom, where you see a small bookshelf attached to the ceiling, and ah, yes, the stripper pole. He spins around it, shows you some of the stuff he's been practicing. When his girlfriend arrives, everyone eats. Ryan has been cooking "oden" (which you and everyone else mistakes for "Odin." *What? You're making a Norse god?*). It's a fish soup, lots of "fish hot dogs" (as Heather, Ryan's girlfriend, calls them). You eat the oden and almost moan. It's delicious. Oden with a hard-boiled egg, a cup of sake. "You ever try it with this?" asks Ryan and he pours some scotch whiskey in your glass. You hammer down the sake and soup, offhandedly mention that you're having girl problems. "What kind of girl problems?" inquires the cook across from you (he looks like Daniel Radcliffe). "I think she's fucking someone else," you say. "What evidence do you have that she's fucking someone else?" "None. No evidence." "I wouldn't worry about it then." Grace stays home, the rest of you head out to drink more sake at a sushi restaurant. You are watching black and white samurai films and you tell Ryan that hot sake is your favorite smell. You munch on small seaweed chips and crunchy wasabi balls, not really thinking too much (you're drunk). Grace comes to pick everyone up. "Wanna go roller skating?" asks Ryan, and you say you can't (it's true, you're supposed to meet Jan later). You walk through a bookstore and don't say anything because you're drunk. That's a lie, you see someone you like, an older guy named Jack and you shoot the shit with him for a moment before going outside and shooting the shit with Bella and then you saunter down to another bar and order a beer. Jan is late (she's always late), you're drunk and the beer goes down easy. You send an email to Claire on your phone, you put your cigarettes in front of you (almost as a dare), but you don't smoke any. Inside, you stare at the window (Jan is late, Jan is late). There she is, you see her coming across the street. You walk her to the park where you first kissed, you tell her that you are confused. You aren't quite sure exactly what the conversation was about. Something about how she's always late. Something about you being worried that she doesn't want to date you.

Something like that. You aren't actually worried that she is fucking someone else (that's a lie, but you don't bring this up as a point). You tell her all this stuff and you collect your things from her apartment and walk home.

~

You wake up in the middle of the night and make hot chocolate. Ramen. You sit in your usual spot by the window, you are one step away from yourself. You are not there.

~

You bike in the rain (light mist).

~

*Inject your eye contact directly into my veins,* you think as she looks at you.

~

Early morning cafe, playful classical music on vinyl. It is still dark out. A man with face tattoos sits outside with his large, paper cup of coffee, scrolls through his phone, smokes a cigarette.

~

"Vitamin B, man, you need to get some vitamin B if that whiskey is still hurtin' ya," winks the Cowboy from back home. The Cowboy was a regular at your old cafe, came in from time to time to use the Wi-Fi, to chat you up. "What's Portland like?" you ask him. "I love it, man. The vibes are good. I think you would dig it. Like, once I step foot in a city, I think it's easy to tell whether or not I'll like it. It's immediately clear. Like San Francisco: it's dead. Can't stand that city. Maybe at one time it was cool, but…" his voice trails off, he shakes his head. "I love Oakland. I liked Seattle, I like a lot of places. My wife and I drive around in an Airstream together and we sort of follow the vibes." He goes on, but you are lost in the idea of Portland. *The vibes are good, the vibes are good, the vibes are good.*

~

You are with Jan, you tell her that Portland is for healing (you tell a lot of people that Portland is where you came to pick up the pieces, Portland is where you came to try and get better, to stand up and become an adult).

~

You show Jan some of the things you are writing. She points at a line, a quote from a friend that you scribbled down. *I think you are a good person who tries his hardest to be an asshole.* "Is that about you?" Jan asks. "Yes," you say quietly.

~

*In a drunken passion I unfriended Jan on Facebook last night.* This is what you tell yourself, this is how you are going to explain to her. You aren't sure if it's humbling or what. You are too proud to friend request her now, in the early a.m. She will notice. She might be hurt. You have all your things back, if she wants them they are here for her.

~

Jan is what it feels like to lose someone. Jan is the person that you are afraid of most.

~

You check your pockets, but you quickly realize that's not where your heart is.

~

The man outside smokes his second cigarette.

~

*Grocery shopping,* you think calmly. *I will grocery shop. My life is not falling apart.*

~

*Ah, there it is,* you think to yourself. *The fear is back.* It grows like wings. Here are your horns. Here is the cigarette protruding from your mouth. Here is the rap music blaring in your ears. Here is the belief that you don't need anyone. You are hunched over, walking through the snow (there is no snow). "My daddy taught me you don't need nobody," sings Isaiah Rashad.

~

It's cold as balls out. Yesterday you were soaked, your gloves were wet, they just made your hands colder. *Home, home, home,* it's all you wanted as you biked along the white river. *Cold cold cold.* When you are cold you dream of your sheets. When you are alone you think of Jan. *She is leaving you, do you know this?* says something in your head. *Shut the fuck up,* you reply.

~

"Sounds like she dumped you," your sister tells you over the phone.

~

"You should make her mashed potatoes. Like, everyone gets flowers or teddy bears when they are apologizing. You gotta be original. Get her some mashed potatoes. Safeway is like a block away."

~

"Please text me back to let me know you have received my text messages." You wait with your phone face up on the table while you read. You wait with your phone face down on the table while you read. You check every so often, turn the phone over, and she hasn't texted back.

~

You don't know if it's premature to start thinking about this relationship in the past tense. You settle for doing so, just because of how angry you are, angry that she isn't texting back, angry that she was always late, hurt because it feels like you weren't enough. You are drinking orange juice in a cafe reading Patti Smith and you are going to download Isaiah Rashad's album onto your Spotify account (because "Cilvia Demo" is the soundtrack to being alone) and "haunt" around, smoking cigarettes and being surly. You can do whatever you want, fine, this is great (it's not great), you would rather date someone who respected your time (is this working? All the self-help wisdom you've read, all the stuff that pulled you through middle school). It is, it's kind of working. You think of Ryan's soup, and conclude that if Jan is not going to text you back, you might as well check in with some other friends. *Yes*, you think, *some company right now would be good.*

~

Jan broke up with you via text message. You spent a lot of today biking around Portland, very angrily. Jan broke up with you via text message. The details don't seem to matter. You bundled yourself in your bed as you often do when you get sad. She reported that you are needy, that you need a therapist. You disagree. Sometimes. But having someone tell you what to do, no, it never sits well. Neither does getting dumped. Over text messages. You have unfriended her over all forms of social media (at this point in your life, you are very good at this, it is almost second nature). You hurt again. Your heart feels like it is imploding, it feels like it is creaking at the sides. You struggle to plug the holes with Christmas wrap and scotch tape. *Merry Christmas, Happy Fall,* the ship is sinking and you are drenched.

~

"What's bad for the heart is good for art," writes Jandy Nelson. This has become your mantra. Maybe you will finish this novel, this memoir, early. All the stuff you write, you feel like it has the potential to hurt someone. You never want to hurt anyone. All you want is to write the truth, your truth. You are not here to cause pain. You are here to speak what's on your mind, to save someone (who?).

~

"You should see a therapist," Jan texts you. "She's right," your friend Parish texts you. "I mean, everyone should really be seeing a therapist." You disagree. What part of you needs to change? *What is bad for the heart is good for art.*

~

*Dear God be good to me. For the sea is so wide, and my boat, so small.*

~

Your heart feels like it is a tin shed with a black hole inside of it. It crumples, your eyes and ears lock to the flapping part of the tin shed's roof, as it peels inwards towards the black hole.

~

So much of your life is *repairing* this hole. So much of your life is navigating through the fog. You haven't looked at Monet's painting in a while. You pull it up on your screen (you jerk yourself off a little bit, *yeah, I have a recurring motif, FUCK ME FUCK ME*). You look at it quickly, you want to think "eh, whatever," but you can't. Here is what you think instead: *hushed, hungry, soft paddle dips, a distance seagull, a fearful child, a fearful father, who does his best not to appear so.*

~

There is a moment when you feel better, your mood will change. You know that you are silly, you might be a fool, but you think you do everything in your power to be honest and true. You have flaws. You aren't perfect. You are broken. But you limp forward with a great enthusiasm. *Love!* you croak and cackle as you limp towards the sun. All the way proclaiming love and scaring all of the passerby.

~

"She's a bitch," says Parish. "I don't know. I don't think I'm allowed to say things like that," you say. Parish huffs. "That's fine. But I'm allowed to say all the things that you can't say. And what I am saying, is that she was a bitch."

~

"So, is Parish your side piece?" asks Jim. "I am uncomfortable with the phrase 'side piece'." "Is she your sidekick?" "I think that's more accurate."

~

"I'm just gonna date dudes," you mutter to Parish, but you don't think she notices.

~

There is a moment when you are eating pineapple because you have had really weird body odor and you think that eating fruits and veggies will improve the way you smell. It's like, you know, an investment.

~

Your friend John works in the tech industry and he jerks off in their bathroom because, "the toilets are fucking heated." He sighs, looks at you across the table, over his coffee, his fingers rest on the corners of his eyes. "Like, after seeing *Wolf of Wall Street*, it sort of like, gave me permission to start jerking off at work."

~

"You need to see a therapist," said Jan.

~

"Punch me in the face," says Ben. You hit him as hard as you can in the jaw. Later you are drinking beers with Hank, and you brag, you say, "Yeah, punched Ben in the face earlier," and Hank shrugs, says, "What? Am I supposed to congratulate you for being masculine?"

~

Sometimes writing feels like holding up a mirror to your face and screaming into it.

~

*I'm allowed to make mistakes, I'm allowed to make mistakes, I'm allowed to make mistakes.*

~

You press your hand against the mirror, look yourself in the eye and beg yourself to come.

~

"Like, if you had a clone, would you fuck him or what?" asks Kevin. "All I'm saying is that if I ran into an exact duplicate of myself, I would fuck the shit out of that guy. And he would fuck the shit out of me, it would just be *phenomenal* sex."

~

Claire e-mails you, tells you that you are "mean." It's like throwing a balled piece of paper at a police officer, or a tree. "Mean?" You are much more than mean. You are hunched over. You light a cigarette. Cars pass.

~

Bullets in your left shoulder. A clock chimes somewhere (it's not a clock, it's just a coffee grinder).

~

In your journal somewhere, scrawled with what looks like crayon, are the words, "Is this the sound of a melting brain?"

~

You have read that beginning Buddhists meditate on the idea of their corpse decaying and returning to the Earth. They are asked to meditate on this idea for a long time. You want to say a year. You can't remember. When you stand behind the espresso machine with your half-smile and do all the stuff that Thich Nhat Hanh tells you to do, sometimes you meditate on the idea of your own rotting corpse.

~

*Get dark, get weird, dig me out.*

~

You are afraid of yourself sometimes. You think your family is afraid of you too. The man to be most afraid of is the man who has nothing to lose. You hold the mirror up to your face, your hands bleed, *WHAT DO YOU HAVE TO LOSE* someone screams.

~

You think about peeling your face back and all that there is too see are black maggots.

~

You check your pockets for your heart, it's not there (you left your cigarettes at home). You open up your jacket and look in your chest. Your heart isn't there either. *The boat,* you realize. All the hairs stand on your neck, you run from your job, from work, people yelp as you push them aside, *no no no,* you make it to the dock and the horn sounds and you can see your glowing heart (in a wooden box with latches), it is being loaded into the captain's cabin. You run to the edge of the dock and jump onto the ship, security personnel rush at you from all directions, but thank God you are on the boat with your heart, even though it isn't directly in your hands. You whisper a prayer, *Dear God, be good to me. For the sea is so wide, and my boat, so small.*

~

In *Impression, Sunrise,* you were convinced that something

115

was burning, but it was just the early morning fog.

~

You lie awake and stare at Xavier.

~

You feel freed by the idea that we do not choose who we love. You aren't sure if it is true. It definitely feels nice to think, but you are wary of anything that feels nice.

~

You are going to get new glasses once your healthcare kicks in. Rimless, Steve-Jobs-esque glasses. it's gonna be fucking great. You are planning to jerk off to your reflection. You had a friend in college who used to pose nude in front of his mirror and eat pears. This may have been a rumor, but he never tried to stop anyone from talking about it.

~

"I have a theory about people," your supervisor at your coffee job tells you one day. "That if you look at anyone at all, you know, attractive or not, tall or short, whatever, if you look at someone, odds are that they are either farting, thinking about sex, or both."

~

Here is your heart. It was in your pocket the whole time. Hold it three feet in front of you. Hand it to someone else (never hand it to someone else).

~

Here is your heart. Keep it safe. Whisper "good morning" to it. Teach it how to walk.

~

The sun is rising. You rub the crust from your eyes and turn on the kettle (you smell, you should eat more fruit).

~

Sometimes you feel like explaining yourself is exhausting.

~

Sometimes what actually happens is more complicated (and much more boring) than what can be translated onto paper.

~

Sometimes you are afraid that you lean towards doing erratic and extravagant things because all you want is attention (all you want is attention).

~

Last night you spoke with Jan. The details aren't lascivious. You sat down in a bar with Jan and realized that there had been a miscommunication. You are still "broken up."

~

Sometimes your body hurts. Sometimes you can't see straight.

~

This morning you are in pain.

~

You are still angry at Jan, despite the fact that you are now on "good terms." The details do not interest you. You are still angry when you see her come up on Facebook. You have re-friended her out of a courtesy.

~

You have a lot of books to read (books books books).

~

Claire called you last night from out of the country. While you were at the bar with Jan, Claire called you last night from out of the country. "I can only talk for three minutes because this is very expensive," she said.

~

"Oh no," she said. "We've been talking for ten minutes."

~

Yesterday you woke up not knowing how much would happen in one day.

~

Last night you sat on your floor trying to think of a way to write about happiness in a way that wasn't sappy (you couldn't do it). You were very happy that you heard from so many people that you loved.

~

Are you hungover or did you just not get enough sleep? Or, perhaps, are your dishes just not that clean.

~

*Go home.*

~

You should do yoga or something. You are still angry at Jan.

~

You tell Jan that the novel is going well, you tell her that you have mixed feelings about publishing it. "Maybe you should burn it," she says. You laugh.

~

You are angry, you hope it has to do something with not having enough caffeine or not having enough cigarettes. Or maybe you just stayed out too late last night (it was a Monday for crying out loud).

~

So old. You're so old.

~

Jan looks at you like she is still in love with you (this makes you angry).

~

"Why do you punish me for loving you?" asks Claire.

~

You want to burn down the "mature adult thing." You don't want to do the "mature adult thing." Right now you have no reason to like the "mature adult thing." You loathe the "mature adult thing."

~

At church small group, a friend of yours always cringes
when someone accidentally uses the word "hate."

~

Last night you didn't dream. You woke up feeling shitty.
You were afraid that upon opening your laptop in the cafe
that the windows from your porn sites would still be open.
This is an absurd notion, you still feared it.

~

You want to win Jan back (you don't want to win Jan
back).

~

You had drinks with someone new last night (are you
ready for the heartache? Are you ready to do this again?).

~

*Hand me a pen or a paintbrush, hand me your hand for a moment,*
*hand me my heart if you have found it (this last part is a joke).*

~

*I AM SMARTER THAN EVERYONE ELSE,* a tiny
monster in the back of your head yells. *YOU'RE*
*WRONG,* someone yells back.

~

You are in a cafe, your fingers smell like dish soap, and you drum them on your upper lip and try to decide whether or not this novel will be a masterpiece or a death sentence.

~

*It's not that bad.*

~

"Too many books," says Jan, tapping her head.

~

Here come the screams again, the chainsaws.

~

You need yoga or something.

~

Last night you go to a poetry reading and you cheer a little too loudly for a girl you like. This morning your back hurts. Everything hurts. You need to improve your posture. Jan, last night, showed your where your chakras live. You are still angry at Jan. You have not had enough caffeine.

~

In this moment, you do not care too much about
*Impression, Sunrise.*

~

In this moment, you do not care too much about love.

~

In this moment, you are trying to drink water, to caffeinate
yourself, to identify the location of this body pain. You
need healthcare. Or yoga. Or vegetables. Or something.

~

You have a lot of books to read. You have a lot of work to
do (what happened, last night you were so in love with
everything, you were so thankful for the day). Maybe you
sleep funny. Maybe your toothbrush has weird cultures
growing on it. Maybe you are dying (you aren't dying).

~

*Wake me up.*

~

What have you learned?

~

You try to love as much as you can. You try and bundle up and repair as much as you can. *Hiding. Hiding.*

~

Claire's writing is impressive. She sends you e-mails and they are the best things you've ever read.

~

Here is your pain. You can get rid of it easily. You have to shed it like snakeskin (is this the correct metaphor?). It is not like your heart If you kept your pain close, it would corrode the edges of your heart.

~

"Don't keep your pain a secret" (that's from one of your middle-school self-help books).

~

*Wake up, it's time to go to work.*

~

You tell Jan over drinks that you think that the writing is going well, that this novel is really exciting and has potential (you believe this, but you will never know unless you share it with someone).

~

*Wake me up, please.*

# 6
## MAGNUM OPUS

You are sitting in a cafe, someone is hammering on the wall behind you, someone is doing dishes. Your lower back hurts, your throat hurts, you want to be in love with life again, but your hands are dry and water feels strange to drink.

~

*Monet, where are you?*

~

You google "where is Monet buried?" Monet is buried, replies Google, in the Giverny Church Cemetery. There are photos. You recognize the place from his paintings.

~

You are not Monet.

~

*Give me your chainsaw mouth, give me your face tattoo, carve a hole and spray me with splinters.*

~

You are trying your best. This is the saddest part. This is the part that makes you think that you are doing okay. Better. Whatever. It doesn't matter. You are doing your best. You can say that confidently. You are not lazy. You are driven, punctual, on time, creative (ugh), you are becoming a better listener. You are doing okay. You are trying your best.

~

In acting class, your professor used to ask everyone to hug themselves during warm ups. Lily used to say it was her favorite part of the warm up. *So often we forget to hug ourselves.*

~

You are cheesy. You are maudlin. You are right. You are wrong. What you want is always impossible, but you do it anyway.

~

*I love you.*

~

You are hurting inside.

~

*I love you.*

~

You are listening to a voice and it isn't God.

~

*I'm allowed to make mistakes.*

~

There is a moment when you are sitting alone in a cafe again. *Fuck Patti Smith and her fucking book,* you think (*M-Train*). The book is pointless, it's her just hanging out in coffee shops and musing about her past. Sure, it's a little fun to read but what's the fucking point, it's fluff.

~

*You are fluff.*

~

"STOP."

~

Your shipmates are afraid, you are yelling into the fog, holding your hair at your temples with your fists. *Where is Jan where is Jan where is Jan.*

~

"STOP," you yell into the fog again (there is no echo, there is no dry land, your crew is afraid and it is your fault). It is here, at the bow of the ship, that you begin to weep. You wish that Ben could punch you in the face a thousand times until you are bleeding into the hull of the ship. You wish that you could've kissed Xavier. You wish that you could've told Claire that you loved her. That's it, you are looking at your fingers (they are dripping with blood), and Ben (in this dream, he is your first mate), he is standing over you, waiting to see if you want him to continue punching you. This is true friendship. He would kill you if you asked. But instead you tell him to stop.

~

On the ship, it is cold, and it is morning. The sun is red but you can see it (alas, a constant). Your heart is where it should be. Not three feet in front of you. Not buried under lock and key in the cabin of the ship. It is here in your chest. And you whisper to it softly, *shhh,* because it is so afraid, and so are you.

~

*Dear God, be good to me. For the sea is so wide, and my boat so small.*

~

"How are you?" your sister asks. "Meh," you say, texting back. Your heart pangs. "Talk to me," she asks. "I'm going to write instead," you reply.

~

You have started smoking cigarettes again.

~

Kindness breeds more kindness (each cliché is a like a chainsaw).

~

*You are loved.*

~

Stop.

~

Today you Googled "magnum opus." It is the most important work of an artist. It is their seminal piece. Who decides what is the artist's most important work? Aren't you the judge, if all of the self-help books were right as they slowly stroked your ego and told you that you were a God?

~

You want your life to be your magnum opus. Whether you like it or not, your life will always be your magnum opus.

~

Here is a small flower. Here is a passing car. Here is a child staring into his reflection, or out the window, it is hard to tell.

~

*Love me. Love me.*

~

November has been hard, you aren't sure if it treated you well. If you died tomorrow, perhaps November would have been your magnum opus.

~

Here is a small flower that you offer up to the sun. Here is a silly gesture. It is only silly if it feels silly (*please, take this flower*).

~

You hate everything. You are stressed and smoking cigarettes. Spending money on booze. Filling out paperwork. Worried you aren't going to make deadlines for your writing. Really anxious. And sad because of Jan. It's a fucking shitshow. You need to talk to someone.

~

You are only writing breakup poems. You are feeling like you want to cry every time you have a cup of coffee. You are trying to "feel what you need to feel." Angry. Again. You are smoking cigarettes. You have $1.75 in your bank account. It feels better to spell it out: a dollar seventy-five. A dollar FUCKING seventy-five.

~

You are thankful for friends (it is almost Thanksgiving).

~

How smart are you?

~

It is almost Thanksgiving (you are alive).

~

You have a dollar seventy-five in your bank account.

~

Stress. Stressed. Cigarettes.

~

You need to send Claire an e-mail, you have to do paperwork. You are irritated still. You like walking around, listening to rap music, and looking as angry as possible.

~

You could make a long list of the people you love. You typed out their names then backspaced. Love hurts you, love floods your heart (it isn't caffeine this time). It is morning and you feel like your heart is full of love that bleeds so much that you need to hold your face in your hands. *Please do not tell me what I am feeling is wrong.*

~

You are reading *Adulting* by Kelly Williams Brown and you hate all of the advice she has on how to interact with people. You are convinced that the way you behave at work will get you fired. It does not bother you that much. You are convinced that you will not live that long. You are trying to grasp onto something solid (a memory, an image), you want to write something *good* but it may not happen this morning. All you have is this love that hits you like rapid fire, fifteen images of people who have made a positive change in your life, *here come the tears*.

~

There is a moment when you are sitting in a cafe with your friend Vincent, and he tells you that no person is more intelligent than the other in the grand scheme of things.

~

It is not even ten a.m. yet and all you want to do is sob into your bedsheet

~

"You should see a therapist."

~

Writing as therapy. Art as therapy. Reading as therapy. Love as therapy (or a destroyer). Where is Claire, where is Claire, where is Claire (out of the country, beyond our borders).

~

There is a moment you realize you are still in last place in your fantasy football league.

~

There is a moment you want to be held by something, even if it is just your drool-stained comforter.

~

Your internet subscription renewed on your phone last night (PORN!).

~

You want to wrap yourself as tightly as you can in your drool-stained comforter. You want soup. You want "that warm fuzzy feeling" but it isn't there. Maybe this isn't love you feel. Perhaps it is just an ache.

~

Biking in the rain.

~

Here is a moment: your sister, maybe three or four, with a nose that bleeds all over the front of her shirt, and she doesn't know what it is, she walks to your father and says that her "hands are dirty," and Dad freaks out (internally) upon the sight of the blood, but manages to calmly bring your sister to the bathroom where he cleans the blood off her and plugs the hole. How many of us are bleeding and don't realize it? ("Daddy, my hands are dirty").

~

You are sitting at home with a bottle of whiskey under your pillow, watching *It's Always Sunny in Philadelphia*. You are kissing Hannah in her car on the edge of the Bay. You are kissing Maya while Claire is texting you. You are leaning over to Xavier and telling him that you want to kiss him. You are crying in the snow in front of your dormitory. You are getting drunk with Ben. You are writing alone in cafes. You are in love (or so it feels). You are in your dorm room the night before you leave college (Claire won't let you sleep). "You're not allowed to sleep," she tells you. Your friends are carrying you home as you cry in your arms, telling them that no one loves you. You are pointing and laughing at homeless people in New York. You are crying on a fence and Lindsay puts her hand on your back. You are on a rooftop in Brooklyn telling everyone that your name is "Jody." You are in a car with Brian, driving on the wrong side of the road, blowing through stop-signs. You are in a diner with Jan, she stares at a painting over your shoulder. You are in a diner with Claire, the two of you eat in silence.

~

"You feel too much," says Jan.

~

"They say that travel does things to you, if you are a writer. So I'm like, 'Please, do all the things to me'."

~

Will you ever feel good, or perfect? Sometimes you do. You are always suspicious of this feeling.

# 7
# CIGARETTES

You and Ben hunch over in the Christmas wind and attempt to smoke Lucky Strikes because you saw them in *Mad Men*. Ben had to watch YouTube videos to try and figure out how to smoke them, you are both baffled by the fact that it has no filter. "You gotta hold it in your teeth," he says, trying to show you.

~

Your father told you that he smoked cigarettes once, and he was afraid of how good it made him feel, so he never did it again.

~

You are easily distracted. You keep on flitting back to Facebook to see how many likes you've gotten on a photo. You think about how your friend Daniel constantly criticizes himself for little things like this, and all you want him to do is thrive. You want to be an example, you want to do everything that others can't. Nick Flynn is teaching a writer's workshop in Oregon in January. You are trying to assemble the poems you are proud of (someone told you that he isn't teaching the poetry workshop). You don't care too much. You need a cigarette. Correction: you *want* a cigarette. You've been having a cigarette or two a day. Your healthcare kicks in soon. Where are the beautiful moments? Who loves you for who you are?

~

You are dancing sometimes. When you are alone, waking up, listening to music. You have to do this. You have to be okay even when you are afraid that things aren't. Emotions are messy, *assemble me into something beautiful*, again you are dancing (you try to imagine dancing and crying at the same time, you can't).

~

You should do Tai Chi or something.

~

You are dancing at the slow shifts at the cafe. You are dancing across from your co-worker. On break he passes you and makes a gun out of his hand and deep-throats it.

~

"A friend once told me that just by knowing that I exist, she feels less alone. Isn't that great? Isn't that why we should exist in the first place?" If this work means anything, it is hopefully to make someone feel less alone. Is that the grand meaning of everything? Existential questions don't matter. You are lost. You take a deep breath, look down into your empty coffee cup, try to think of something to say, something to contribute to your magnum opus. You want to exude wellness. You want to heal someone. You want to alleviate human suffering. If you have a home in your heart, you can invite others in.

~

Why do you like Monet so much? You think it makes you feel sophisticated (*ooo, look at me, I like art*). But you sincerely like Monet. You like good books, you shouldn't feel bad about it. Go ahead, have the courage to like Monet. The colors, the scale, the soft melancholy of the paintings. How everything is slightly blurred. You want to develop a relationship with Monet and his paintings. Why not?

~

You again think about that quote by Marianne Williamson, "Our deepest fear is not that we are inadequate, our deepest fear is that we are powerful beyond measure."

~

Two weeks ago you took someone else's order at a burger

place on purpose. You bragged about it to a co-worker, he told you that you were, in sum, an asshole for taking food that someone else paid for. You tried not to care. You went home early from work that day.

~

"It is our Light, not our Darkness, that most frightens us."

~

You are broken, you are trying to heal. Water and Portland and bike rides and opening your heart. All the silly but necessary things. You have blushed more in the past month than you have in three years.

~

Blushing is a tell that what you are feeling is true.

~

What are your truths?

~

"Your errors," says Nietzsche.

~

Do not feel guilty about the things you know.

~

Hardship. Heartship.

~

"Why you carry boulders by yourself?" asks Isaiah Rashad.

~

There is a moment when you doubt yourself. There is a moment when you stretch your arms out and realize you have been hunched over your laptop for a good couple hours, trying to capture love and maybe missing it. You twist left, then right, trying to correct a knot in your back, thinking about another cup of coffee, or maybe a cigarette, trying to escape the self-loathing, trying to say some nice things about yourself. A dollar fucking seventy-five. You sigh, shake your head, and do a little jig. Check in with your back. Your heart. You try and think about that ship, the one in your imagination that is going through the fog with Ben and Nick Flynn, but the truth is that you are in a cafe and you don't have any money and you are fine because you are not dead. That is the gift. Here is a cliché. Here is a cup of water. Here is a bowl of soup. Here are a handful of people that love you. Here is a God that loves you (you smirk). Here is you being okay with everything, with acknowledging you are lucky.

~

You have a lot of work to do.

~

You can only be yourself.

~

You check your watch. "Yeah, I can shit out a couple more clichés in the next hour, or for the next week."

~

*Stop.*

~

Do you feel less alone?

~

You have taken to praying for your friends when you are sitting at slow shifts at your job.

~

Perhaps by praying for your friends, they will feel less alone and not know why. Perhaps a prayer will change their day.

~

"I pray for you sometimes. Just so you know," your old

pastor tells you in a coffee shop. You and your family say "vibes" instead of "prayer." You send each other "positive vibes." Your father often "sends you strength."

~

You had your cigarette, you had your coffee. You feel a little anxious, a little on edge, which you realize was probably the point. Maybe you will mellow out later. You picked up *Challenger Deep* and read the afterward and it scared you. Sometimes you worry that you suffer from mental illness. You worry a lot. A lot of your day is focusing on breathing. You are very self-conscious. Perhaps you should dance more. You are in a different cafe, drinking water, staring at the Buffalo Exchange across the street, trying to check in with your breaths (you spent two minutes skimming some Thich Nhat Hanh this morning) and you are seriously considering therapy. What would you tell the therapist? Perhaps that you are anxious a lot, so much that you go home from work sometimes. Part of you doesn't want the help, part of you thinks you will be fine, but then why do you pray? Why do you go to church? Because human beings are all here to help each other, right? You draft an e-mail to Claire, who called you two days ago, then delete it. You drink water and you conclude that everything is alright. You are excited for Thanksgiving, you are planning to make a pie or a Filipino dish. Your brain bounces from idea to idea and you blame the internet, you blame phones. You are always afraid when you do not feel like you are in control of your body. Sometimes when you are stressed, it feels like you are standing on the edge of something, or like you are about to fall down a flight of stairs. The last time you went to the doctor, he told you that you just needed to "exercise" and to "spend time with friends." More exercise: sure. You have a dollar seventy-five in your bank account. A cigarette, you aren't sure if it is a proper way to combat or medicate stress. It isn't, it really isn't, you conclude. Stress plus cigarettes equals heart disease. You sigh, look out the window again, just in time to see a man walk by with a cigarette in his fingers (he blows out the smoke, mixed with normal breath condensation). A cigarette is an excuse to go outside. A cigarette is something to do. A cigarette, you believe, is just part of life when you are in a metropolitan area.

~

As an artist, you do not need to be mentally ill. You do not need to be tortured. You just need to be willing to feel and explore the complex and oftentimes scary world of emotions. You want courage, you pray for this.

~

The night you told your family about what happened at school, when you came to health services and told Daniel's mom that you wanted to kill yourself. That night your parents let you stay in bed with them (you were a junior in high school), and they asked you what was wrong and you told them "a combination of things." They held you and you stayed in bed with them for a while, then went to your room and slept. It was around this time you started reading *Nox* by Anne Carson, a book that changed you.

Collections of scraps, photos, translations. Your parents were afraid for you, they were afraid because the book seemed to suggest that one of the characters committed suicide, they hoped that the book wouldn't fan your flames. You brought this up with your therapist and she laughed, said that your parents were overbearing. Your parents didn't like hearing this. They wondered if you should continue seeing Dr. K.

~

The tightness in your chest is back. Perhaps you should stop smoking cigarettes this much (one or two daily). It used to be only two or three a week. Now that Jan is gone, it feels fine to smoke cigarettes. It's a growing addiction, it grows each time you return to it. Vance says it makes him sad whenever he sees you smoking on your Instagram. Sometimes you take pictures of your ashtray. One time in Vance's car, a lighter fell out of your pocket.

~

"There's something a little bit off about you," Kate says lovingly.

~

You want to be more lucid. You want to go about your day and not be afraid that the world is going to end. However, you aren't sure if this is the right way of thinking. *Sigh.* You check in with your heart, it is silent. You check with your cup of water (it is silent). You check

Facebook and your phone. Nothing. Last night you got drinks with Ryan and wrote poems over beers. Last night you expressed your worries with Vincent about writing. Last night you missed Jan but you didn't message her. Today you sat in your apartment and tried to read Thich Nhat Hanh, but instead you went out for a cigarette.

~

"What's your biggest fear?" asks Jeff. You take a breath. "My apartment burning down. And household chemicals. What about you?" "Glitter and balloons," he says solemnly. "I'm dead serious."

~

You are going to be okay.

~

Some day you will quit writing (?) or not. You love it. Maybe you will change your genre. Maybe you will make music. Maybe you will pain. You almost laugh and think about Monet. *You are not Monet*. You didn't dance in your apartment this morning. You tidied up a little. Cooked a meal. Perhaps instead of writing right now, you should be sleeping. Typically, Tuesdays are a little difficult for you. You always spread yourself too thin, you underestimate how long your workday will be.

# 8
# DRUNK

There is a moment when you tell Tiffany that you think French is sexy, she immediately leans into your ear and says something soft, something that you don't understand.

~

This morning you are hungover. You are surprised you made it home. Whenever you get really, really drunk, you suddenly become very active on social media. Selfies, comments, you're all over it. Yesterday at work you had a splitting headache after a day of being customer servicey. Being nice for too long gives you a headache. Right now you are in your usual spot in the cafe and you are staring across at the Buffalo Exchange again and you try to calculate if you have enough time for a nap. You think you might even still be a little drunk from last night, because you are wearing a stupid hat that your sister gave you, but you don't really care because it feels dope to wear it (it's

147

one of those knitted bomber hats with tassels). You are drinking water and blowing your nose. You hope your novel is nothing like *M-Train*. You are confident that you did not like *M-Train* at all.

~

You probably don't have a tolerance anymore. You had four drinks last night and you still feel drunk. Three is the recommended dose? You aren't sure. You scroll through the texts you sent out to girls from work, and you are knocking over things when you get up to refill your water cup in the cafe (still dizzy). You have work in four hours and that is definitely enough time to take a nap (you need a nap), and you need to eat lunch and you have this whole list of things that you need to do. Like e-mail Claire. Like un-hangover yourself. Water. When you hold your mind-mirror up to yourself, you conclude that you shouldn't have spent that much money on drinks last night. You have done okay this month, but last night you did, indeed, make a mistake, money-wise. It was fun though, you had a good time (what are the consequences?).

~

It is sunny today in Portland. You are wobbly and lucid and the sun shines brightly (in its "early-morning" way) through the buildings, and you think about how sunrises feel and look different from sunsets.

~

You hope you can pull it together before work today. Gat-damn, you think about how Chet used to get hammered and then puke at work. You aren't gonna puke at work. You are just gonna feel like shit. And you have drinks tonight with Henry. Fuuuck.

~

You want to get a full length mirror so you can dance in front of it. You want a heavy coat. You want a San Francisco Giants baseball cap. You need to take a shit at some point. You need a nap.

~

There is a moment where you are sitting in a cafe (again) kind of hungover and trying to put yourself together in the hours you have before work. You are going to take a shit and something tells you that it is going to be a little bit of a sloppy one, that's the price you pay. You didn't even drink that much. *Who are you?* you think to yourself, shaking your head and bringing the cup to your lips again. Water. Tomorrow is Thanksgiving and you want to make a pie. You don't know how to make a pie. You don't even know how many ingredients you need to buy. As far as Thanksgiving is concerned, you think you are a little bit screwed. Tomorrow you are going to show up with your friend Parish (who everyone thinks you are dating), and you will either be holding a store-bought pie or something that you put together last minute (*no, this will not happen*, you promise yourself).

~

Your shit was not as messy as you thought it would be.

~

You have a window open in your computer, an empty e-mail draft with Claire's name in the "To:" box. You think about being healthy (yoga, fruit, exercise, saving money). You review what you have written so far and you are very happy with it. You have noticed that the mornings after you are drunk, you feel mentally sound. You enjoy sitting here in relative peace and typing out something that you are confident is art (*HIGH ART*, a voice in your head screams) and you chuckle and sigh and wonder how you are going to get through eight hours of work today.

~

Justin is nice, quiet, sat next to you in the bar last night and bought you whiskey shots. You are at peace possibly because you lobotomized yourself with whiskey and tequila. You rise for another cup of water, yawn, and weave through the maze of chairs in the cafe. There are no chainsaws in your head today.

~

You listen for the chatter that is usually careening at a thousand miles an hour in your head but none of it is there. Silence. Peace.

~

You reach out and hold Jan's hands, you play with her fingers. you pinch her wrists. It gives you so much satisfaction to see that she still looks at your snapchats (*GOOD*, you think, *let her see what she is missing*). She is only missing out on you being alone. You furrow your eyebrows. You look at the cars and people passing by, the Buffalo Exchange stands solid and unmoving like a church. You can see your reflection in the glass only if you really try.

~

Jan still has her childhood teddy bear. The teddy bear has holes from all the love it has received. Gus's bear is also like this. He is twenty-two and still has his childhood teddy bear. You notice that all the things people love (stuffed animals, books, articles of clothing) deteriorate from use. Unloved objects, perhaps then, live longer.

~

You hold up this mirror to your face and your hands are no longer bleeding, you are not screaming at the mirror, you are just tired, and a tired reflection stares back.

~

Sometimes you want to hold yourself like a comfort object. You sometimes feel like you are your own teddy bear. If you could divide yourself into two people, perhaps

you and your clone would just go home, nap, and hold
each other.

~

You are convinced that this novel is one of the better
things you have ever written. You are very happy with it.
Just a couple days ago you were sure it was garbage. *Silly
brain*, you think. *Where did all this doubt come from?* Your brain
is so messy. All you want to do is hold it. *Awww, c'mere*, and
you hold yourself and then suddenly cry because it feels
like home.

~

Thanksgiving is tomorrow and everyone thinks you are
dating Parish. You brought this up with her, she laughs.
"But we're such good friends, can't a guy and a girl be
friends? It's rare, to have a friendship like this." "Yeah,"
you say back, unsure, but whatever, you like getting drinks
with Parish, you don't necessarily have to be dating. It's a
good friendship. And everyone thinks you are dating her.

~

You need to get home to your nap. You are worried that
you aren't going to make it. You always avoid going home
when you aren't sleeping or eating. But you need to do
both. You like going home. You need to go home. You are
really into the idea of getting cozy. You will not call out of
work today, even though the thought enters your mind
and it is seductive (you imagine a tiny hula dancer, this is

how you conceptualize the idea of calling out sick from work, "Call out sick!" sings the tiny hula dancer in a cartoonish sing-song voice). You won't. You push the hula dancer out of your mind and sit at the cafe and look at the harsh, cold reality of the table in front of you and the early morning light and the chatter of the cafe and your heart full of love. There is so much love there. It surprises you.

~

When you live in the same place for a while, you stop seeing things. Your routine makes everything blur together into a blob. You go on autopilot (it's nice, relaxing to be on autopilot, as long as you are aware on autopilot). After settling into a routine, you will forget things (like your keys, like turning off your stove, like the exact location of certain shops), you will sort of *lock in* to new things that appear, because that is your brain's job, to make habits (sustainable ones) and to identify threats and change. You look across the street next to the Buffalo Exchange and there is a tree (it's an aspen tree). When you were smaller your father would point to aspen trees with glee and say, "Look! They're waving at us!" because the tiny leaves flutter. The aspen tree across the street is waving at you.

~

Fuck everything. Fuck this Thanksgiving bullshit. You imagine publishing this online. It's your own little act of pyromania, it's your own little arson. Fuck this. Fuck everything. You have to make a pie. In your bag you have the evaporated milk that you forgot to buy yesterday. You might be running late. You don't care. The anger is back, is here, sitting in a different cafe, taking down an espresso and trying to think how you are going to put this motherfucking pie together. You spoke with Lars last night, who writes journals like you do, who fears publishing them above anything else. You have to publish this. Unedited, unabridged. You will have Vincent write the forward. You consider having it password protected for a month. You need a second set of eyes. You want to make this fucking pie. You want to eat some food, go home, clean everything. You want to finish this book, to publish it, to believe that all the shit you hammer out onto the page, all the stuff you squeeze out of your mind-cock, you hope that it means something. None of this matters.

~

There is a moment you are scrolling through your phone. When you were drunk last night you texted Jan. When you were drunk last night you texted Beth. When you were drunk last night you changed your profile picture.

~

You are trying to figure out what to do about this book, now that you are so close to finishing it. A couple more days, a couple more thousand words. You need to sit down with Vincent. You need to do something. You need to have a deadline. You just need to get your work out there in the world before you die. Humans, right? Their achievements are so impressive, so full of passion, because of their short life spans. Let us do something grand, let us flash brightly once, let us jerk off into the sunset, let us love without an expectation of return, let's become hoarders, let's become arsonists, let us stop trying to deny ourselves of our true nature, let's stop being so sensitive, let's realize that the beautiful parts are the broken parts, let's love everything disgusting about us (EAT SHIT). Let us sit at a long dining table with our friends and family and tell everyone to fuck off, that there is no God, that there is no reason to save money, that there is no reason to sit politely in this cafe when your heart is screaming for something more (we always want something more). You want to gather all the huddled people and pass them slips of paper that tell them that they are beautiful, and when they turn the paper over it's a picture of your cock. Fuck. It's Thanksgiving. You have a wooden heart. You have a hope and a loathing. You have your hands in front of you and you type out onto the page hoping that it means something, and even if it doesn't, here it is. You are lost in your head. *IT'S MY HEAD. FUCK OFF.*

~

The chainsaws are back. The hunger is back. The cigarettes fly out of your pocket, almost immediately into the air. You are fueled by caffeine and all the soap and mold that you accidentally ingest. You have these weird skin blemishes that might be cancer. You have wings. You have horns. You have fingers. You are grateful for your fingers, *look!* Look at these fingers that will type out insults and pain. Look at these fingers that will sew together your skin. Look at these fingers that only feel at home here at the laptop, here are the fingers that hold her face when you tell her that you love her.

~

Good morning. Fuck off. Happy Thanksgiving.

~

You have to make a pie. You're going to make the pie and go to church and then go home and destroy everything (or you will clean everything).

~

Fuck Monet.

~

Good morning sunshine, here is how the world will be: enough, good, furious, angry, diamond-like, in the sense that it will be hard, precious, and beautiful. You will be like grass, or soil, or dirt. You must fertilize the world around you, you must be rich in order to help those around you grow. Fuck everything. Sometimes, the richest soil is where the forest has burned down.

~

You scroll through Detroit's Wikipedia page. Your body aches. Your heart caves into itself.

~

You call your mother, she asks you if you want anything for Christmas. You tell her you want a San Francisco Giant's baseball cap. "Why do you want a giant baseball cap?" she asks.

~

There is a moment when you want to run away forever (just never stop running, in the Forest Gump sense). There are moments when you mutter "fuck" under your breath at work, always when you get lost down your thought rabbit hole.

~

You are in your apartment, listening to music on your phone, bundled up in sheets and pajamas.

~

You are angrily throwing together a turkey sandwich.

~

Tonight is payday.

~

*Tell me a secret.*

~

*No.*

~

It will never be perfect, you will never be perfect, which makes every action perfect.

~

Love everything (burn everything).

~

Hold your heart in your hands (just like Grace Paley).

~

You go through phases.

~

Happy Thanksgiving.

~

You want to raise baby birds. Maybe it will teach you something about dealing with people.

~

People send you their poems, their art, and it always feels like they are handing you their children, asking you, "How much is it worth?"

~

A bill. A medical bill from months ago. Long story short, this is a clerical error. You are irritated and it is a holiday and there is no one you can call about this bill. You are worried that the bill will stop you from enjoying holiday festivities. Hopefully once your friends are here, it won't matter, you will be distracted enough. There is nothing you can do about it today. You take deep breaths and try to focus on the present, which is something you struggle with more and more every day. You biked all over Portland yesterday, first to your Church's Thanksgiving, then to a co-worker's Thanksgiving. The best moment was biking home along the river (so often, this is your favorite part of the day). Blue and gold lights on the black of the river. It's hard to keep your eyes on the path because all you want to do is stare at the river. You think about what it would feel like to drive your bike over the edge, into the water. This makes your shoulders tense, you get dizzy just thinking about it. You bike along the river and take a deep breath, trying to inhale its essence (or something like that, you aren't sure). *Happy Thanksgiving.*

# 9

# THE SHIP

A bill. A medical bill from months ago. The bill is overdue
and the company tells you that you have to pay three
hundred and sixty dollars. The deadline is two weeks. The
words "collection agency" echo in your head (oh well, you
think). But you are going to call. There is nothing you can
do today. This, you think, is the worst part. To have a bill
looming over you on a holiday, when everything is closed.
There is nothing you can do today. As far as the bill is
concerned. You are going to do *other* things, like grocery
shop and go see the tree lighting in Pioneer Square. You
cleaned your apartment this morning and you have only
spent four dollars today (on coffee). Last night you made a
pumpkin pie at Parish's house. Last night as you went to
sleep you wondered if you could ever fall in love with
Parish. You wanted to wake up at 7:00 a.m. this morning
but instead you woke up at 10:00 a.m. You vacuumed, you
finally cleaned your sink, you took inventory of your
groceries, you threw away some quinoa. All you want is for

someone to tell you that you are doing a good job. You look up, maybe God will say it (God is doing something else right now, he trusts you to figure this one out on your own). You appreciate God's trust, but still, some reassurance would be nice. You are all dressed up in a tie and a nice shirt. You are all ready for this day, and you are doing a good job. Self-care, self-love.

~

Last night Geoff invited you to move into his house. It's cheap, it's in a good neighborhood, but you will have to say no. Your heart says no. If you are going to move in anywhere, it will be with Parish because the two of you have developed a strong friend-love. (The bill weighs above you, you try to let it go like a balloon).

~

You think about googling "How to not worry about money." You know there is an article somewhere online that is going to calm you down, but for now you are writing, in your usual spot on the cafe, across the street from the Buffalo Exchange. You had dinner with Geoff last night, and he was drunk and kept knocking things over, talked about movies with you, and you listened with your heart. You biked home and your ears stung. You went to sleep after masturbating. You woke up at 10:00 a.m.

~

You do not want to be lobotomized. You want to be "metaphysically equipped." Someone said this last night at Thanksgiving. "I am metaphysically equipped, but as far as actual physical objects, I am not equipped."

~

Here is a small breakfast for you. Here is a small cup of water. Here is the belief that writing will keep you alive, keep you going, keep you thinking that everything is going to be okay (you dare the universe to take you down and the universe laughs a little and says, "If I really wanted to take you down, you'd be gone already, but here's something to keep your Friday interesting").

~

You don't have any desire to look at Monet anymore. All you want is to see your friends in a couple hours, to share a beer or a whiskey, and to watch the tree lighting (the Christmas Tree lighting!). Geoff tells you that he hates Christmas, because his ex-wife *loved* Christmas. You feel sorry for him. You love Christmas, but you know that you don't like Jack Johnson because it is attached to your first high school relationships, and every time a Jack Johnson song comes on you cringe. You can't imagine what it would be like to see a Christmas Tree and cringe like that, to remember the pain of someone cheating on you, on someone packing their things. You try to imagine but you don't know, hopefully you never will. This is why you stay alive (this perhaps is the most compelling reason), but because *tomorrow* is the ultimate mystery box. You have no idea what is going to happen, why turn off the movie early? Maybe this is poor reasoning. You throw it into your tool box.

~

Our ultimate freedom lies in how we choose to see the world. This part of why you have faith in God. However, once God permeates your life, if feels like less of a choice. You are afraid of religion. You walk towards religion, then take two steps back. You wish you had a comfort-object, like a teddy bear or a blanket. You need something to hold onto as you walk towards the irreversible.

~

Here are your beliefs (sometimes they feel silly and brittle) and you want someone to love them as much as you love them. *Here they are, look,* you share your little collection of beliefs. Some people study them, hold them up to the light. Some people make lists of them for future reference. Some people will kneel down with you and admire how much they sparkle.

~

Here are your beliefs, in that small treasure chest that used to contain your heart. You have to pad the edges with newspaper. You keep them tucked away.

~

You are a museum. You are a church. You are (to someone, someday) a home. You straighten the cushions. You vacuum the carpet. You have enough silverware and cups and bowls for two. For now, it is just the waiting (you don't like waiting very much). *It is here for when you get here,* you think.

~

Claire is out of the country. You want to buy her a Christmas gift but you aren't sure where you would mail it to. You can't mail it to her house because her parents know how sad you make her.

~

The past is not set in stone.

~

The heart can change.

~

Tomorrow is a mystery box (you love mystery boxes).

~

A mystery box is a box that you do not open. Its contents are whatever you can imagine (which almost always surpasses what is actually inside). J.J. Abrams has a TED Talk on this. You have a mystery box in your closet (it is your most prized possession). Hannah gave it to you for Christmas four years ago.

~

Your heart and your mind are mystery boxes (what a shame, what shame, because all you want to do is to open both of them).

~

"Here's something that you may not know about me," says Geoff. "I listen to vinyl records. Exclusively." "Noted," you say. "I will start a hashtag: #discoveringGeoff." He shakes his head, doesn't respond, reaches for his wine again.

~

You will sanitize this novel somehow, clean it up, put it online. There is no way you cannot share what you have written. You aren't sure if you should edit it (you should at least give it a once over). It's a sad look outside a cafe window, a cigarette as you walk home from work. The things you gravitate towards when you are reading a book. As long as it comes from a place of *love* (this is the end goal, this is what you want), you will be fine. The messy parts of love and your mind. You want it to be tidy but it won't be. You are not Monet. You are not perfect. Here is the proof. Then take your small, light, brittle beliefs and freak out every time the wind rustles them.

~

Maybe you just get sad in winter. You called out sick to work. You had a nightmare about swimming through day-old soup. Your body aches. Food tastes not-great. You called your father because it is his birthday and he asks you if you are sad because of the breakup and you are but that's not really the issue. Last night you went out drinking with friends. You went out drinking with friends almost every day this week. Today is your punishment. You called out sick from work. You don't want to see anybody. You want to feel normal again. You want to change your name. You are afraid of getting fired for calling out sick (this was part of your stress dream). Whenever you are afraid you are going to get fired, you revamp your resume. It's funny, you always quit jobs before they fire you. You always leave relationships before you are dumped. With some exceptions. You are afraid of making it to the finish line and being deemed incomplete still. An irrational fear. But real. And pressing.

~

You need to buy some stuff. You made a list. Last night you didn't sleep. You read books on military strategy and tried to liken it to your life. You tried to figure out what is important (you often ask this question to yourself: what is important?). You treated everyone to drinks last night. You went home alone, very drunk. You spent a lot of money last night. Though there are worse people in the world than you, you are still ashamed of how you behaved. You are not proud. The evidence is all over the internet. You

retreat to your hole, wrap yourself in blankets, and
mentally identify the pain in your ear, your throat, your
lower back.

~

You sometimes think that you have friends only so that
they will catch you if you fall. Sometimes you feel like it is
so easy for you to slip. You live in a state of high stress
and constant worry (this is the only way you know how to
live).

~

Sometimes people invite you to things. Sam invited you to
do photography projects. You never followed up.
Sometimes you invite people to things. You asked Geoff if
he wanted to get beers. He said yes. He never followed up.

~

You will survive. You know this. Sometimes you aren't
sure. You think it is a silly assumption to believe that
everything is okay, but sometimes you need this silly
assumption in order to do things like your laundry and
make telephone calls about payment plans for your
medical bills.

~

You maybe need more sheets on your bed (you curl into
yourself when you sleep, maybe this is why you have so

much back pain).

~

You think you are a little overqualified for your coffee job.
But it is a job. You are unsure. You are trying to do a
monthly check-in where you assess your goals, your likes,
your skills. None of this feels fulfilling. You want to get
excited about something again, but you know getting
excited about something lasts about a day or two before it
becomes hard work.

~

Maybe you will go back to sleep. Maybe you will read a
book. You called out sick today (if you hadn't called out
sick, you would be working right now).

~

Around this time two years ago, you didn't get out of bed.
You stopped going to class. You woke up and went into
town and read books in cafes. You went out for drinks
every day this week. You are not kind to your body, and
thus your body hurts. *Give me something for the pain,* you
think (it is the lyrics of a song, or an idea, you aren't sure).
*Give me something for the pain.*

~

The coffee just makes you more tired (back to bed, back to
bed).

~

People can't be happy all the time, right? They have to have ups and downs, right? You think about how Buddhists request that you think about throwing a pebble into a still pond. The ripples go everywhere, it eventually returns to stillness. Nothing seems to change.

~

You aren't sure if a cigarette will make you feel better or worse in this moment. Sometimes you are afraid that all the food and water in your house is somehow contaminated, that you are unwittingly poisoning yourself when you cook for yourself.

~

You are going to stay at home today and tidy up. Quietly read books.

~

This morning you are sensitive to smells.

~

Maybe all the pain you feel is just a hangover. Maybe all the pain you have ever felt is just a really big hangover. You are afraid that you are going to get fired. You are afraid you have a mental illness. You are full of worry and fear, you wear it like a suit covered in multi-colored pipe cleaners.

~

A desire to take a shit. A desire to puke a little. A desire to feel better. A twinge in your jaw. You are sometimes afraid that you are going to shit yourself for no reason. You sometimes go to the restroom just to check to see if you have shat yourself and did not realize it. You should see a therapist. It has become a mantra. You don't want to but now you can't shake the idea out of your head. You are going to read more Thich Nhat Hanh. You don't think living should be this difficult (though you often hear that no matter how hard you try, you will always struggle with living, as long as you have a human mind). Bring yourself back. Focus on your breathing. Your anxiety knows no bounds. Turn it into art. Turn it into writing. Sell it for ten dollars (or more if it's "good"). Maybe you will go home. It is 10:07 a.m. and you should be at work right now, but you called out sick.

~

You are afraid of so much, and you don't think that you have to be.

~

Espresso. The pain in your jaw. Healthcare soon.

~

Jan looks at all of your photos on snapchat (you can see this).

~

You post photos of you having fun just so that Jan can see that you are fine (you aren't fine).

~

Claire wants to marry you.

~

You are crying on the ground with Claire sitting across the room. You have an arm extended, you tell her not to move.

~

You withhold your anger. You are afraid of telling people that they are wrong. You are afraid of giving your honest opinion (you are small, sometimes it would be silly to give you honest opinion).

~

Here are your wrists, extended. Here is a loving hand telling you, "No."

~

Here is Claire sending you an e-mail, to tell you that the two of you "belong together." You believe this to be true. You are learning this to be true. You took a lot of convincing. You need a strong story. You need someone who loves you. You can love Claire. You are sure you can.

~

Today is a day for melancholy. It's a good idea that you took the day off, even though you feel a little bit guilty. You stayed home and napped and had nightmares about coming home to an empty apartment. You had dreams that Jan was walking away and you were yelling for her to stop, but for some reason you only could imagine it, you couldn't actually open your mouth and say it. You ate some leftover pasta, had a cigarette on the way to the cafe. No music. "These quiet days are good for you," you scribble in your journal. The cigarette is going to kick in later and you might go bonkers. For now you are mellow, and are still glad you didn't go to work. You repeat this in your head like a mantra. This may be the day that you finish this book. There are times when you just want to finish a project to start the next one. Things are good (why do you always have to remind yourself of this?). You have this tower of fears, things that may or may not happen, you are trying to plan for every outcome, and this planning destroys your present. So much of what you do tries to focus on being *okay*. You don't necessarily have to feel happy. All you want is to feel somewhat safe for the time being. All you want is to feel listened to. You want to feel *worth* something. Who can tell you that you are *worth* something? Is it you, is it God? You ordered tea in the cafe, something caffeine free. You wrote a list of things you want to get done in the cafe. Budgeting, research, trying again to find some purpose.

~

There is a moment when you realize that navigating through the fog is how it will be a lot of the time. You have to sing songs with the crew, bang your fist on the table, celebrate that you haven't died yet. Dances and stories. Weeping together, huddled close.

~

You woke up and cleaned a couple dishes. You picked up some books on military strategy. You read some fiction and fantasized about disappearing, changing your name, just for the thrill of it. Two days you watched a clip from a movie you love, and you realized that the dream is to find the thing you like and to find the thing you are good at. You like writing. People believe that you are a good writer. Writing is such a difficult endeavor, there is no money in it. But you do it because you love it. You want to dig deep and tell people some fundamental life truth, but how on earth can you convince people that their lives mean something when you struggle with this every day too?

~

If you can find a way to keep your fears and anxieties in check, the battle is half won. You brought some Thich

Nhat Hanh with you. You've been spelling his name wrong. You are tired. You have spent most of the day in bed. You are drinking tea because you know that coffee might send you in a direction that you aren't ready for. You want equilibrium, but every time you find equilibrium, you throw more rocks into the pond.

~

*This is something grand, isn't it?* You think, smirking. *This is my magnum opus.*

~

"No matter how close I am with someone I am dating, I would never, ever show them the contents of my journals," says Lars. "Sometimes they'll say, 'Oh, I want to know what's going on in your head,' and I tell them, 'No, no you don't.'"

~

You are thinking of sending e-mails out to your friends. At least Ben, who you miss. Ben who lives several thousand miles away now, Ben who is not close enough to punch you in the face.

~

So many of us write when we are sad. Sometimes we are only driven to read books when we are faced with something we cannot understand on our own.

~

"I have grown skeptical of staring at inkblots," says Lars, in reference to reading.

~

You let Parish down. You were supposed to go to a circus event with her tonight, but nothing feels more wrong for today than a circus.

~

You are a source of joy for some people. You force yourself to think in this direction, it feels like it takes actual physical energy to do this, like lifting a heavy wooden beam and directing it somewhere else (or! steering a ship).

~

There is a moment when you realize that you are happy (despite all of the fears that weigh you down). You are sitting in a cafe, playing hooky (essentially) and working on a novel in a cafe. When you have always dreamed about your life, you always dreamed it to be like this. Here you are! You've made it! Smile for chrissakes.

~

There is a moment when the fog clears for a moment, and there is sunlight. The crew rushes up from the gallows (you were the first to see it, but you didn't even have to yell, the sunlight shone through the slats of the ship) and it renders everyone silent. The sea is vast, there is no sign of land, but the sun is out! The men all close their eyes and bask in it. You join them.

~

You are still unsure of what to do with it. You believe it to be one of the best things you've ever written. If you are going to be honest with yourself. And you smirk a little. That's all you want to be, is honest with yourself.

~

You wring the lemon dry. Your hands hurt. Will you rewrite this? Realistically, no. You will save this uncut draft and revisit it, delete a bunch of parts. You can make it palatable and comfortable, but the fact that this first draft exists, that is the most important part. This was an attempt to put your demons to rest. The hope in the beginning was to get all of you down on paper, all of your heart, all of the roaring, to say *this is me* and print out the final manuscript and hold it to your chest and whisper, "You are a rabid, disgusting man but I love you so much."

~

Because you need this. You need to tell yourself this.

~

Books sustain. Books are magical objects, and you are told that no one reads anymore. But you go to cafes and see people reading all the time. You walk through bookstores and see people light up when they find something interesting. A book is one of many answers. The question is constant and always. Even when books die you will love them as much as you love people.

~

Books are your stepping stones across rivers.

~

Books! You can say more in a book than you can say in a conversation. *Here is me, unedited! Live forever! Live forever!*

~

A sudden change in mood. Your tea is lukewarm. The bills are still there. Your job is still there. Everything is fine (please repeat this forever).

~

There is a moment when you return home and cook something that is kind of edible and you will curl up with a book and wait to work the next day. You have healed from your hangover, and each time you come back from a depression, you hope it will give you enough confidence to climb back out when it returns. You tidy up and turn on the kettle. You clean one dish at a time. You correct your spelling errors.

~

Today is the day you finish the novel. You are in a
Starbucks staring at a Christmas tree. You have been
fighting the sads all day and the sads have been winning.
You aren't much of a football fan but you play fantasy
football with your friends because you love them. You get
sports news on your phone and none of it makes sense to
you. You are drinking bottled water and your throat is
sore. You have a mild headache and you just watched a
Pixar movie. It is dark out and everything is lit with
Christmas lights.

~

There is a moment when you want your life to be a tightly
woven Pixar plot. You want beautiful animation, you want
a harrowing ten-minute opening sequence. You want
people to pay millions of dollars to see you overcome
some obstacle. The movie soothes you because it makes
you believe that this is possible. We pay millions and
millions of dollars because we need to be soothed, we need
to be reassured that love wins. Love does win. Pixar is
selling us water. There is a moment you want your life to
be a tightly woven Pixar plot. You, ungainly, will overcome
your fears. This is what you need to believe. You throw
eleven dollars into the pool of millions and watch the film
and feel like it was worth your money. You walk away
mildly dehydrated and feeling better than you did two
hours before. *Thank you Pixar*, you think to yourself, *take*

*my money, make me feel this way forever.*

~

There is a moment when you are trying to find a way to neatly tie together all the frayed loose ends. There is so much hope. The story isn't done. You cannot cut and trim, because your life is like an open box of live wires. You cannot snip any of them or else you would lose something. Here is the box that is your heart. Here is the wire that is your love for Claire. Here is the wire that is your love for Jan. Here is the wire that is your love for Xavier. Here is the wire that makes you feel like you are worth something (you are always ready to snip this one).

~

There is a moment when you realize it will always be this way. There are moments where you will see the sun. There is a moment when your friend Ben will uppercut you in the jaw and you will taste your own blood and you will think, "Yes, that was good."

~

It will only get darker, you will one day die. You sit on the bow of the ship and hum solemnly.

~

Different times of day. Varying forms of light.

~

Here is your heart. Here is your tangled heart. Here is your arm, three feet or so, which you hold out your heart unflinchingly and say, "Look." This is your show. This is your guide.

~

*FINISH IT,* screams a video game character. *NO,* you scream back.

~

There is a moment when you are standing in front of David's mother, telling her that you want to die. There is a moment where you are crying in the snow and you want to move to Canada. All of these painful moments, they hang above you like the Northern Lights.

~

Your bike is at home. You cannot bike along the Willamette. You look around you and somehow you find the Starbucks to be beautiful. Despite the sore throat, despite your headache. Yes, this is home, this is thirty percent battery on your phone on your laptop, this is how it will always be, and God is here, around us, and you say this confidently, and the fear is nowhere to be found.

~

There is a moment when you will check your word count, and see if you have reached your goal. And it will mean something. And you will print out the manuscript and place it on your dinner table and give it a long, hard look.

~

YOU ARE A GENIUS.

~

YOU ARE A MAN.

~

HERE ARE THE SOUNDS OF DRUMS.

~

HERE ARE THE CHAINSAWS. THE SCREAMING, THE CHRISTMAS CAROLS. YOU DESIRE EVERYTHING. YOU ASK FOR MORE. YOU, WITH GRAND SWEEPING GESTURES, PRESENT YOUR TESTICLES TO THE CROWD AND SHOUT, "HERE THEY ARE YOU FUCKERS."

~

Your hands are cold.

~

You now understand what Claire means when she tells you that you are not allowed to die. You now understand what Claire means when she tells you that you are not allowed to die. *I am allowed to make mistakes. I am allowed to make mistakes. I am allowed to make mistakes. I am allowed to make mistakes. I am allowed to make mistakes. I am allowed to make mistakes.* You repeat it fifty times as you round a corner. You repeat it fifty more times as you stand behind the espresso machine at work. You say it into your reflection as you hold the mirror with both hands bleeding.

~

You are going to compose a letter to Claire. It is not the right answer. But she will like hearing from you. You haven't written too much about Claire, which you don't feel too bad about. You wrote a fair share about Jan, but Jan doesn't get the letter. You have all of Claire's notes and paintings in a shoebox beneath your bed. You are never sure if Claire is the answer, but she is the one that you always return to. *But won't it be a good story?* she says. You need this. You need this. You need this. It is not the right answer. But you want it to be. You are shouting at her with your hand out, as if to protect her. You look away and cry and shake.

~

Jan runs circles around you, pretending to be a dog.

~

Xavier sleeps, his hand in front of you.

~

*Wake up. Wake up.*

~

You think that all of this is going to end, that credits will roll, but they won't.

~

Your breath smells terrible.

~

Your fingers are cold.

~

You point at your heart. You want to say something silly but you can't.

~

You are out of words. You are looking around the Starbucks for fodder, for something to fill this empty space. You look around you and keep looking. Amidst the iPhones and the little red cups and the puffy down vests and the startling amount of tourists, you keep looking.

# SPECIAL THANKS

Erin Miller
Jonathan van Belle
Bobby Eversmann
Zac Doege
Lucas Brandt
Megan Johnson
Luke Fraser
Isaiah Rashad

# ABOUT THE AUTHOR

Connor Miller is a writer and performer living in Portland. He has written the novel *Thomas* (2015) and the poetry chapbook *Pain Parade* (2013). You can find more of his work at connorthemiller.wordpress.com.